The Sex Club Murders
and Other Kinky Tales

Second Edition

Published by The Nazca Plains Corporation
Las Vegas, Nevada
2008

ISBN: 978-1-934625-16-3

Published by

The Nazca Plains Corporation ®
4640 Paradise Rd, Suite 141
Las Vegas NV 89109-8000

PUBLISHER'S NOTE
The Sex Club Murders and Other Kinky Tales is a work of fiction created wholly by *Markus Larsen's* imagination. All characters are fictional and any resemblance to any persons living or deceased is purely by accident. No portion of this book reflects any real person or events.

Cover, Fleshblack Images
Art Director, Blake Stephens

Dedication

I would like to dedicate this book to Tim Brough, whose help advice, love and support thoughout the years has been nothing short of invaluable. Also I wish to thank Stephen Nelson, Lee Grupsmith, House of Behrmeister, Master Cain Berlinger, Master Alex Keppeler and Household Keppeler, Andrew Masterson and Bears Like Us and all the perverts male and female, gay and straight, whom I have had the pleasure of calling family and friends.

Yours in leather,

The kinky cub
Markus Larsen

The Sex Club Murders

and Other Kinky Tales

Second Edition

Markus Larsen

CONTENTS

INTRODUCTION

Leather is a journey. Mine began almost thirty years ago. Until I was 16, BDSM was pure fantasy. I was Prometheus tied to the rocks and surrounded by impenetrable fire. Tarzan or Bomba stripped of my loincloth and tied expertly to the chair and tortured. I served as personal slave to the mighty musclegods of Mt. Olympus ever under the watchful eye of Zeus and Vulcan, the well muscled machinist made of Zeus' thunderbolts. It wasn't until I was 16, a junior in high school, when I got tied up for the first time. I was nervous until the first of the ropes touched my wrist and ankles. It was pure electricity mixed with fear. I became naked, powerless, and tied to his bed. He, Vic by name, was older than I. He was all of 30. He explored my body with his hands, his tongue, and the hair of his beard with an erotic touch, that I had never experienced before. It has been a long time since then. When I was laying in my bed at my parent's home, if you had told me of the experiences that wait from play – flogging, caning, play piercing, catheters, sounds, bootlicking, bootblacking... and the marvelous people those came with, I probably would have not believed you. This cub has been lucky in many of the wonderful people who have share their lives, loves, friendships and perversions with me. To these wonderful individuals, club brothers, and leather households, my heart will also be full of respect and gratitude to all.

Leather is a journey. Take one step at all time and one day at a time.

Always do your best, be honest with your limitations, but be proud of the good things you have done, be good to the good people around you, and always have a good time. The hard-learned lesson for me was learning that not everything in the leather community is so damn crucial. If it doesn't get done in this moment, it will be done in the next. I've panicked and worried over things that on reflection weren't all that important. I've worried that people might not like me or that I might not get a chance to play or learn. Relax and take it one step at a time. It will happen.

Now I get to share my greatest passion with you, my writing. My intentions in this book were to create an anthology of tales that would not only titillate but also entertain. If this cub has lead you astray or made you laugh within all the eroticism, I am glad.

The slave 7 mysteries have been a long time in coming. I fully realize that is tinkering in a major way with the Master/slave dynamic. That was part of the joy of writing about Master and 7. Taking what was already an interesting dynamic and throwing in that Master does not want 7 hiding behind him but going forward to get involved with what is going on and then thrusting him in the limelight to be involved in the solution. Master wants his slave in trouble which in itself is far from the original dynamic but not so far that Master is not able to exert control. In this way, 7 is His Master's puppet. His adventures are entertainment for His Master. They feed some base sadistic need to watch His slave overcome evil and even death all for the glorification of Himself and in service to Him.

Dick Strong came to me when I was writing this book. Actually, I intended him for a gay publication that I later decided not to submit him for. The adventure though fun had no kinky elements and I like him better with boy, Jason, in tow. This was my first attempt to write noir, a genre that is usually charged with endless heterosexual innuendo. I enjoyed bringing him into the gay world and the world of kink as well. Most noir detectives spend their time getting beat up anyway. Time one should enjoy pain instead of always shaking it away and escaping from it.

Here's to the best of times as you go on your journey. Remember not everyone's is the same. Take what turns you on and embrace it as part of the being that you are. Your road is taken at your own speed. Learn, experience, and enjoy!

If you find the time, drop me note. I can be found at thekinkycub@aol. com or at www.aderangedmind.com.

Until we meet again...

Yours in leather,

Markus Larsen
The Kinky Cub

A Boner Book

THE SEX CLUB MURDERS
CHAPTER ONE
ANOTHER SATURDAY NIGHT

Master leans over glaring from His seat on the bed.

"Now lace up the other boot, slave."

It is a privilege to rub my hands along Sir's knee high, oil- tanned leather Carolina's while binding Him into them. The smell of the leather mixes with His own personal musk. I slowly lace up Sir's boots, making sure to pull them tightly but not too tightly that they should be too snug for him. This slave can feel under the smooth soft leather the hard muscle of Sir's hairy leg. When I reach the top holes, He pulls the laces tight, makes a knot, and then a small bow. He then tucks the ends into the boot. "Okay, pig. Now take that little hard-on and go put it in a pair of pants." I crawl over to the two trunks on the far wall of Sir's walk-in closet. One is an old yellow steamer trunk with drawers. From one drawer, I pull out a neatly folded T-shirt with The Anchor insignia and from another drawer a pair of black socks. The other trunk is an old battered khaki army trunk. It has the pants and the leather this slave has earned. All is neatly folded in its inner sections. From this trunk, I pulled a pair of jeans and a black leather jockstrap. Sir picked up both trunks at an old resale shop just before I was allowed to move in. Sir allows the slave only three pairs of shoes - a pair of boots, a pair of black dress shoes for work, and a pair of black walking gym shoes. They get shined and cleaned weekly after I finish doing Sir's leather. As

I pull the boots out from under the bed, Master rubs His hand over the slave's ass then gives it a hard, single swat. "Thank you, Sir. Sir, One, Sir?" He smiles down and lightly slaps my face. "Always ready for me to use you more, aren't you, slave?" Saturdays are usually when I give the house a more thorough cleaning. Today, Sir decided differently. He saw me on my knees scrubbing the floor with my round butt up in the air. That may have done it. Sir dragged this slave down to the dungeon and threw me at the base of the St. Andrew's cross. This slave lay there crumbled in a heap. He kicked me repeatedly with His big heavy work boots over my chest, legs, and butt and then pulled me by my metal slave collar and threw me against the cross. The wrist restraints went on and I became his punching bag. Sir makes me do double reps to make sure my pecs are good and hard for times like this when He can use them for His personal punching pleasure. I do my best to keep its chest thrust out because if it doesn't it gets a slap of the balls to remind it. One Master once asked why he doesn't castrate me. Sir said because he likes to see me squirm too much. The imprints of His fists are still on my chest and I can feel them burn as I lean over to tie the laces on the black workman boots. Master takes His motorcycle jacket and throws it over his shoulder. He throws another motorcycle coat down on the floor and I quickly slip it on. Master heads toward the front door and the black and chrome Dodge Ram truck waiting to take Him and His slave on the weekly journey. I check the doors and windows and shut off the lights. As Sir goes to the truck, I lock the door. He gets in the truck and I hand him His keys back. This is a ritual that we do every Saturday night when we are in town. The black truck hums as we pull out of the driveway. The chrome brightly glints short glimmers reflecting the streetlights as we go by. Don't have to ask where we are going. It is another Saturday night and we are going to The Anchor.

Master acquired me about 5 years ago. The slave was allowed to move in after a year. About eight months later, Master officially made me His. The brand on this slave's right butt cheek is a number 7, the slave's Master given name. My birth name is never used as I am a home slave and do not work except for Master's happiness. In addition, there's a chrome chain with a small silver lock. The key was broken in the lock in front of witnesses during an anniversary party at The Anchor. It is a great honor to serve Sir and keep His house and truck. By the way, in case you're wondering, I have been permitted within the last year to start referring to itself in the first person tense, especially when writing these mysteries though I don't always do so. Master says that he prefers that the groveling be saved for Him. Sometimes I still refer to myself as "me", "it", or "itself". Hard for me now to think of me as a separate person. My body, mind, love, and soul are for Him and Him alone.

CHAPTER TWO
THE ANCHOR

Martin Reinders open the first Anchor in the early 1970's in the glow of the Vietnam War. This is his third place with the name of The Anchor and, as this slave is often told by Master, the best one. The Anchor itself is a long, cavernous place with many twists, turns, rooms, floors, stairs, and long hallways. It can be best described as parts bar, bathhouse, dungeon play space, and labyrinth. It is housed in the remains of an old four floor Masonic Lodge in a more run-down part of the north side of Chicago, the Uptown neighborhood, a neighborhood better known for fleabag hotels, auto repair shops, motorcycle chopshops, and mental homes. A sign a few blocks over says, "Welcome to New Chinatown", but this neighborhood is better known as "Little Vietnam" because it is home to a large Vietnamese and Taiwanese community. The Anchor shares the same city block area with a couple restaurants (one Mexican and one Vietnamese), a veterinarian, a small tattoo, piercing and leather shop and a few other gay bars (The Bistro, a combination restaurant and a foo-foo drink video bar, Clark's, a formally loud tropically colored gay billiards bar which burned about a week ago, and Different Folks, a dimly lit wood paneled bar that just got busted for drug dealing and serving liquor to minors again.)

Needless to say, that in the last fifteen years of this location's existence, The Anchor has seen a lot of change. Walls for rooms have gone up and down many times. What was open space was created as more labyrinthine space. Men sodomize and dominate each other in spaces where lodge brothers once spoke in whispers and exchanged secret handshakes. What there is left of the threadbare carpet has been ground into a sort of murky, brownish grayish color. Music from loud speakers fill the background. Mixture of modern pop Gregorian chants, new age, techno instrumental repetitive disco, orchestral, and butch rock anthems ("Born To Be Wild", "Wild Thing", "Hell-bent for Leather", "Born To Run", "Do You Think I'm Sexy") absorb the screams of pleasure and pain and fill the calm spaces. The music gives a rhythm and feeling to the lustful, adventurous, ominous quality of the place.

The entrance is a plain blackened glass door with the numbers "5226" in tan colored, wood grained numbers above it. There is no other writing. The glass door is inset into the building a couple feet and has a plain concrete stoop in front of it. It is one of those nondescript doors that if you were walking along the avenue, you wouldn't know what it was the entrance to or probably never give it a thought as there is no sign above it.

The door leads into a small bluish cracked tiled room with a long caged window. On the opposite wall is a mirror and below it stacks of the latest gay news rags. Behind the counter is usually some pimply-faced adolescent who gives Master no respect and back talk. I used to resent him doing that but then realized he gives the same treatment to everyone who enters. Might catch him later in the night taking his turn at cleaning bathhouse rooms and dungeon spaces or in the futile act of vacuuming the carpeting. Behind him sits wire racks of various packaged condoms and dildos, bags of clothespins, various lubes in all sort of size bottles, balls of ropes, various cheaply made paddles and crops and "room deodorizers". Tonight, the pimply boy is Jim Lattimer. Jim is thin with arms like pipe cleaners. He gives Master a snide smile.

"Evening Jimmy. How's Daddy Barry?"

Jim mumbles "fine".

Jim is boy, to Barry Wilmot, the manager of The Anchor. Usually Jim is following him around like a long lost puppy dog except when he is stuck on the desk. Master's leather shirt stretches tightly over His muscular chest and hairs spill out from the open lacing at the neck. With His massive right arm, bristling with black curly fur and taut musculature. He takes out our membership cards from His upper left pocket and holds them firmly out to the attendant. Jim hits a few buttons on the old green screen computer in front of him and brings up on our account. Master signs us in on that night's sign-in sheet. Then Jim pushes a button under the counter. As it starts to buzz, I run for the door and open it. Master enters and I follow. As I turn to go in, Jim shoots me a revolted smirk and scowls onto the next customer.

A Boner Book

CHAPTER THREE
INSIDE THE DOOR

Just inside the door is the coat check. The slave removes Master's leather jacket, smelling as it does of smoke, leather and Master's sweat, and checks it with the clothes the slave was wearing. Master likes His slave to wear nothing but His collar and lock, leather jockstrap, and rolled down socks over the low black leather workman's boots. Before the slave hands in Master's motorcycle jacket, Master unsnaps the left epaulet and removes the black leather dog leash. From the coat's right pocket, He removes a pair of worn leather restraints and two double-ended hooks. The leash is one handle with three ends each with a hook. Master hooks one to the slave collar and one to each captive tit ring. Then putting a leather restraint on each of my wrists, Master hooks my hands behind my back with a double-ended hook. He leaves the other double-ended hook to dangle off the slave collar.

Just beyond the coat check is a small bar area. Along the back wall is a collage from various leather events and bars from all over the world. Along the bar itself is a row of black leather covered stools studded along the bottom edge of the seat. Under the bar railing, "o" rings are drilled in every five feet. Master walks over to the bar and pats me on the shoulder. This is Master's sign for me to kneel. He hooks the other end of the hook hanging off the collar to an "o" ring. He orders a beer and a bottle of water. Behind the bar, Tim smiles showing his crooked broken teeth from behind his long bushy mustache. Tim serves drinks almost on automatic while inquiring how Master is tonight. Over in the corner, Jerry the bootblack is setting up his old-fashioned barber chair for another night of bootblacking and bootlicking. His shirt is off and his defined abs flex behind the tight hair that covers his chest and stomach. His slim body looks as if he was poured into his extremely short torn blue jean shorts which when he bends over leave very little to the imagination. Glancing over, Master notices the bootblack chair is empty. Master unhooks the collar and motions for me to crawl over to it and kneel. He climbs into the chair and puts his feet solidly on the shoe forms. Jerry smiles.

"7 going to help get the boots clean tonight Sir?" Jerry asks.

Master nods his approval. Master leans back in the chair. I begin at the toe of his left boot and work my way with small hard massaging swirls of my tongue around to the front of the boot around the sole and starting up the shaft. I can taste His man sweat. The smell of the sweat and the leather drive me on to lick longer and harder. Sir begins to squirm in the chair. His gloved hand rests on His knee near His crotch. I slowly work my way up the shaft of the boot and try to make my way to Sir's pants. At the same time, Jerry the bootblack, is worshipping Sir's right boot. I come around the shaft and down to the toe, I glance at Jerry. He is matching me lick for lick. He sees me looking at him and winks. Master begins to rub his crotch and I watch the bulge begin to grow between licking sessions.

Master unzips his fly. He pulls my head off his boot, he shoves his cock down my throat. Jerry switches to my boot and I deep throat Sir's cock. A couple more minutes and Sir lets go a creamy stream of cum down my throat. He releases my head and catching Jerry's eye says it is time to get the rest of the boot cleaning done. I lick the last few drops off Sir's cock. He tucks his cock away. Jerry pouts and then cleans and oils Master boots. I kneel and wait. Master climbs off the chair, zips his fly, tips Jerry, and pats me on the head. Leading me crawling, He walks over to the bar and orders another beer.

Daddy Don Simpson walks away from the coat check storing his check tag in his wallet. The wallet returns to his left back pocket, chain swinging against his hip. He sways and swaggers as he walks toward us. Daddy Don is a furry bear of a man with a large belly, slightly balding head, thick trimmed beard that hangs as below his neck and usually a sunny disposition. Master smiles as he approached and offers to buy him a beer and Daddy Don accepts. He bends down and pats the slave on the head. This slave can smell the stench of stale smoke and spilled beer. "It must be nice to always have such a good, obedient boy," Daddy Don says.

Master coolly answers "it has uses". Master puts the bottle of water to my lips and I am allowed a few gulps before it is taken away. Master finishes His beer and calls Tim to order Him and Daddy Don more. I can't hear Tim as he whispers to Master but I know that Tim usually does that to the person buying for someone who has had already too much. Tim leaves to get the beer. As he walks away, Daddy Don leans his hand on his head. Master turns to him and puts his arm around him. Daddy Don begins to sniffle. "He shouldn't have been there." Daddy Don looks up into Master's eyes. "I'm very sorry. It is hard realizing that Greg's not here anymore. That he died the way he did. Sorry. You have always been nice to Me. I shouldn't bother you with my problems." Master's other hand finds it way to the back of my neck and starts rubbing. The beer arrives and Daddy Don grabs his by the long neck and starts to gulp it down. He slams the empty bottle back down and throws a couple bucks from his chain wallet on to the bar. While thanking Sir for the beer, Daddy Don tries to get off the barstool. He trembles a little bit but gets his balance. He pulls a red hankie from the inside of his pants pocket and mops his eyes and forehead. Daddy Don glances up at Master and puts his arm on Master and announces that he is pleased to find "a friend like him in these times but he needs to be alone". We watch as Daddy Don sways and stumbles his way out of the bar and further into the complex.

Master takes his hand from my head. He leaves a tip on the bar and puts the bottle of water to this slave's lips one more time before leaving it half full on the bar. He taps my shoulder again and I rise to my feet. Tim wishes Him a good evening as we also continue deeper into the complex.

The beat of Grace Jones and "Slave To The Rhythm" comes out of the wall speakers as Master leads slave down the winding hallways.

Screams of pain mix with heavy thuds. Whip cracks mix with the beat of the disco music. Chains clank. The temperature gets warmer and you can smell the sweat and perspiration. In one of the room we pass, a slave is counting swats. "Sir, 24, Sir. Sir, 25, Sir. Sir, 26, Sir."

At the end of this first hall, there is a doorless room with a sign of the same style of lettering as over the entrance to The Anchor. The smaller tan wood grained letters have been glued against a black leather remnant background. They read, "Welcome To The Pit".

CHAPTER FOUR
WELCOME TO THE PIT

As Master leads His slave through the door, we descend a small jog of very narrow stairs. To the right is a brass engraved sign on a stand that reads "Dungeonmaster on Duty". Under the words is a small black plastic sign with a name in white letters on it swinging from a pair of small brass hooks. Master Bill McGuinn is on duty.

The walls of the Pit are covered in black tarpaulin making them and the lofted ceiling look even more cavernous and daunting. The Pit's vaulted ceiling has been painted matte black. The room is lit with overhead caged covered lamps with aluminum foil covering their tops. Looking up as we enter, a pair of saran wrapped bottoms facing away from each other and tied with duct tape are being hoisted up on a hook. Two flogging scenes are going on crosses in far corners of the room. At a floating table, a Top and bottom are in the middle of a candle wax scene with the slave restrained to the holes in the table by rope bonds. A chained and locked bondage boy shivers standing up in a locked cage in another corner. The locks keeping him in chains gleam from the light. And there in the middle of it is Master Bill McGuinn.

Sandy red hair appears from under his Master's cap, tipped at a jaunty angle. He stands there with his massive arms folded, freckled and hairy, smugly taking in the room. Like a large proud Irish bull surveying all his cows, Master Bill walks slowly, as he steps in his knee high Wescos, observing the activity going on around him. He wears no shirt and his clipped chest hair and his slight belly peek out between his leather vest dotted with various run and club friendship pins. On his back is a "Leather Demons of Dante" back patch slightly dirty from age and underneath a myriad of smaller patches from the years of attendance for that organization's weeklong event, Purgatory. Master McGuinn turns around and his eyes land on us.

With a nod of his head, he walks up to Master, extending his hand. Master shakes the offered hand. And Master McGuinn responds with a large devilish smile, a slap on the shoulder while asking in his thick Irish brogue "How the hell have you been?" and begins to chat up Master while offering Him a cage for me. I can't hear Master's answers, but Master Bill nods saying "That's good. That's real good." Indicating the chained boy, he smiles and says, "That's my latest."

He leads Master and slave over to a tall cabinet against a wall. The cabinet is full of latex gloves, paper towels, Crisco, spray bottles of hydrogen peroxide, Simple Green and alcohol and other cleaning and play supplies. This slave kneels at Master's boots. Without taking His eyes off Master McGuinn, Master unzips His fly. Pushing my head, He shoves His hard veined cock into my mouth. His golden piss fills my mouth and streams down my throat more delicious than nectar. This slave gratefully almost greedily accepts the sweet ambrosia. The almondy smell fills my nostrils. Do my best to relax my throat to accept it all. When Master's bladder is empty, He pulls out His soft cock and puts it back into His pants, zippering them. Looking up at Him, I thank Sir. Master McGuinn looks down and patting the slave on the head says, "Did we take our Master's piss like a good little boy?" Master pats the slave on the shoulder. This slave returns to one step behind Master and Master pulls my head on to His shoulder and starts to pat and stroke it.

"Glad to hear all is going well for you then, Bill."

Master McGuinn grimaces at Master.

"Not everything. It is that blasted boy of Martin's. You know. The brat he leaves in charge of this place. I swear if Barry gets in my way one more time, I'm going to tie his sorry little ass to that cross and he'll learn what true pain is."

In His own style, Master reminds him that what we do is not punishment. Master McGuinn growls back:

"Well then, he's just got something coming to him. Make no mistake about that."

Master shakes His head and says we should let Master McGuinn get back to work. The slave take its' head off Master's shoulder. Master McGuinn punches Master in the arm and says that he'll "see you later". Master tugs on the leash and slave straightens up feeling a sudden terrific rush of pain. Master McGuinn tips his cap as Master and slave leave the Pit behind.

CHAPTER FIVE
THE MUSIC ROOM

The exit from the Pit leads into a confusing tangle of hallways, sets of lockers, stairs, and an endless array of doors. The black halls lead past a second set of lockers and separate dungeon rooms, each room with one piece of equipment. Some are occupied, some are not. One large room has a glass window through which shiny, silver fitness equipment can be seen. The fitness equipment is there so The Anchor can legally qualify as a "bar/health club". Another hallway leads into a small cubby with food and pop vending machines.

Rows and rows of plain bathhouse rooms with a single thin mattress on a wooden platform for a bed and another wooden block with an ashtray for a table. Single uncovered red light bulbs light the bathhouse rooms. Some have TVs hanging from the wall next to the door that has multi-channels of porn movies. Master leads the slave through the shadowy and dimly lit halls, passing men in various states of undress, some just wearing towels. The music of speakers has moved on to an extended remix of Gloria Gaynor's "I Will Survive". Occasionally we pass other Masters and slaves. Some slaves are standing next to the Master, some are kneeling, some being given the gift to suck their Master's dick, some being paddled, some licking boots. Throughout the hall is little bars serving beer and a few bottles of hard liquor. A few people stand around them chatting also in various states of dress. Boys kneel at several of these men's feet. A couple of the boys are serving to hold their Sir's drinks while the Sir chats.

From one of the long black hallways, we walk up a set of stairs and emerge into a large room. A huge disco ball hangs from the ceiling and is irradiating its glow over the stained brown tiled floor like a strange silver moon. Loud dance music vibrates a pulse in the warm air of the room, but nobody dances in The Music Room. The dance, if you can call it that, is one of sensuality and extreme horniness.

Across the brown tiled floor are deep mats covered in black cloth. Naked gyrating bodies suck, fuck, lick, and feel their ways around on these mats. Hairy bodies mix with smooth. Slim and muscular entangle among the grunts and groans of pleasure. All is dark, shadows, low groans and perspiration except for one small-lit poster on the edge of the dance floor.

The framed poster shows an old woman with her hair tied back into a bun wearing a flowered house dress and white house slippers shaking her finger at a young boy with the tagline, "Now don't forget to wear your rubbers." On the perimeter are body pillows, cushions, couches, large pillows, and floor mats. Bodies can be made out in the shadow. The area along the wall is in a murky darkness being removed from the light of the ball. On one end of the room, a go go boy who couldn't be more than 22 or 23, too skinny, and still a little pimply shakes his toothpick arms and bony body in time with the music. He is wearing nothing but a leather thong. He has a white towel around his neck to rub down his body with to try to look erotic. His facial expression registers total boredom. Master and slave walk around the edge of the piles of wriggling human bodies each looking like they are earthworms trying to devour their mates. Sweat glints off many strong arms and round buttocks. The slave glances up. In the corner sits a lone man, fully dressed man. He seems detached from the goings on. Master and slave continue to circle being careful not to step on discarded wrappers from condoms and lube. Something by his side that seems to glint in the dark. The man is in shadow so it is hard to make out what little less features of the man himself. Not sure why I am staring at him but I do.

As Master walks around the circle, He senses His slave tensing up. Gathering the leash in His hand, He pulls me to Him. I wince in the rush of pain as it goes through my body as I get closer to Master. The man begins to rise and the object shines brighter.

"What's wrong, 7? Getting turned on?"

The slave fumbles. "No, Sir. It's just..."

Master turns and looks the slave squarely in the eyes. "Just what?"

"Knife?"

He follows my eyes over to the lone figure. Master sees the glint and lets go of the leash.

"Good boy."

Master turns on his heels and walks quickly toward the mysterious man ordering the slave to stay at least two steps behind. The man, judging Master's quick approach, starts to walk away. Master moves faster and have to half-sprint to keep up. The man turns the corner back into the hallway with Master closing in fast. Master turns and skids into the hallway and nobody. The man's gone.

CHAPTER SIX
THE CATACOMBS

Master grasps the leash once again and we walk deeper into the complex. Going down a sharp incline and turning down even steeper set of stairs, we come across a large metal door. Scrawled across the door in orange fluorescent spray paint is "Enter at Your Own Risk". This is The Catacombs. The Catacombs back track underneath the hallways we just traveled and end up somewhere under the street connecting with an unused old fashioned cobblestone sub-basement that Mr. Reinders cleared out for use of the patrons. The sub-basement is the common point but there sometimes seems to be a million ways to get there. Long black tunnels that interconnect with each other like a maze of messy, tangled spaghetti. Lit by small electric lights and strings of light bars across the floor. Time seems to lose itself here along with the Tops and bottoms. Hallways end as suddenly as they begin. In the dead ends, there is a lone piece of dungeon equipment. Pillories, crosses, examination tables, tables floating from chains on a frame, hanging slings, small wading pools, and cages appear at the end of these dead ends. Some of the dead ends have no equipment, but mats, mattresses or air mattresses with piles of bodies in varied acts – group sex, fisting, water sports. Each corner twist and turn is something different, something sensual, almost dangerous and erotic.

A brighter light and we emerge into the sub basement. Brick and cobblestone seem to swirl we enter the tubular space. It smells of water because water condenses off the large metal pipes that hang off the roof of the sub basement. In the background a pump continues to get rid of water and heaters sound on and off to keep it warm.

The light blinds us as we enter from the darkness but our eyes adjust quickly to the room. Master walks into the room and begins to slowly walk around. A body lies in the middle of the long tube. Master moves to the side of the body. The slave follows. It is the body of a young man lying on face down on the cold stones. He is wearing white tennis shoes, blue jeans, and a red satin jacket that says "The Anchor" and the insignia on the back. Master kneels next to the body and I kneel next to him. Blood is congealed on the back of the head and he is lying in a pool of blood as well.

"Do you know who this is, slave?"

Slowly I look into the face trying not to get the blood on me from under the body.

"I believe, Sir, that this is Barry Wilmot, the manager of The Anchor."

Master feels Barry's wrist then his neck.

"He's dead." Master climbs to his feet. "Wait here, slave. Be back as soon as I can with assistance."

I watch with a sinking feeling in my stomach as Master releases the double-ended hook on the restraints to release my hands and then walk toward the Catacombs and disappears into the dark.

CHAPTER SEVEN
EXAMINATION AND OBSERVATION

Barry's body couldn't have been there long because rigor mortis had not yet set in. His hand felt clammy to the touch. His lips looked almost like he could almost speak. Shivering, I looked around. The body and I are very much alone. Getting up, I look around. A dented heater in the center of the room blasting streams of hot air didn't seem to help. There is only one door. Slowly I open the door standing to the side as it swings open. Inside, there are several wooden shelves filled. The shelves are filled with cleaning supplies. A mop sits in alone in corner net to a yellow rolling plastic bucket and its ringer. As I exit, I notice a couple boxes by the door of paraffin candles and sterno cans. I walk back to the body. The body is starting to stiffen slightly against the cold cobblestones. Steam from it starts to become visible against the cold. Wish Master would return. I return to the body and do my best to examine it without disturbing the evidence. No visible bullet holes. Some blood underneath the head. A nasty bruise on the front of the head, but that could have been when the body fell or was hit... On Barry's right hand is a small silver friendship ring with two hands holding on to a heart. On his wrist, an expensive looking black faced Movado. His gold chain peaks out from the top of his T-shirt.

The slave is about to stand up again when noise comes from the Catacombs. Running feet. The slave runs for the entrance to the sewer to be beside it when they enter and behind the people who come in.

The noise gets louder and louder. Suddenly they rush in and a group of men with an older man with a younger woman struggling to keep up with him stop dead in his tracks on first sight of the body. Master stops just over the body. I rush to get off my place on the wall and a return to Master's side giving his arm a squeeze.

By the time I reach Master, the older man and the woman have joined Master as well. The older gentleman is neatly combed and dresses. On his back he wears a shiny black satin jacket embroidered with the gold letters.

"The Anchor –Owner and Proprietor". Underneath a picture of a sailor like Brad Davis in "Querelle" but this one leans against a very large anchor. The man, Martin Reinders bends over the body of Barry and sweeps it into his arms. Turning it over, he cradles his bloody head like a father holding an infant. Master insists we should call the police. Reinders lays Barry back gently on the ground. Reluctantly agreeing with Master, Reinders slowly backs away from the body his eyes never leaving it. He slowly turns away and mumbles something to the woman from under his bushy white mustache to call the police. She tosses her long brunette hair behind herself and rushes into the Catacombs. Reinders glances back over his shoulder and slowly drags himself back into the darkness of the Catacombs, Master turns to slave.

"Well, Holmes, have we deducted anything?"

The slave looks up at Master smiling.

"A great many things, Sir, but need more information, Sir."

CHAPTER EIGHT
THE CORONER AND THE BROTHER

A slave hears a good many things by being unobtrusive and maintaining silence. I slowly and obtrusively move over to a policeman talking to a older man wearing a long white coat that reads "Coroner" on back. Master watches as I slowly stroll back to them. Here was a chance to help solve a real life mystery and it would entertain Sir for me to do this. Sir jokingly calls the slave "Holmes" because what the slave reads the most is mysteries. Occasionally the slave will pick up a new cookbook with meals to tempt Master's palette or the latest leather play instructional opus or smut novel, but my favorite is mysteries. I get to read them an hour to an hour and a half before bed when Master is sitting in bed alone or in his office relaxing from the day and He doesn't need the slave. But, as soon as the clock on the wall turns 11, Master will need his bed turned down and a slave lying his head on His chest after first making sure that He has everything he needs and He is comfortable. It is fun to spend that hour before in the company of Hercule Poirot, Jane Marple, Kinsey Millhone, Goldie Baer, V.I. Warshawski, Ellery Queen, or slave's personal favorite, Sherlock Holmes. Be sure, however, none of this compares to laying my head on Master's furry chest, being held in His muscular arms and the words, "Good night slave. You will always belong to me."

He has always said "If we get into a mystery, I want you to solve it." Sure Sir was joking, but here we discover a dead body with no apparent killer in sight.

After the paramedics have removed the body, I report to Master what I overheard from the man from the Coroner's office. The Coroner said he wasn't sure how Barry died, but he was sure a rounded instrument like a lead pipe or a screwdriver inflicted blunt force to the back of the head. The coroner estimated that Barry has been dead a little more than an hour. The cop told him that one of the employees had seen Barry enter the Catacombs, he was sure that no one was following him. He watched as Barry disappeared into the darkness. Master leaned up against the stone wall smoking on his stogies. He listened to all that I had to say and then motioned me closer. Ordering me to open my mouth, I was allowed to recycle His cigar smoke by inhaling it in. The white smoke tastes of cherry wood and aged brandy.

Pointing with his cigar, Master draws my attention to a scene in the corner of the long tube. A thin boy, dirty blonde hair hanging in his face tries to light a cigarette, but he has trouble keeping his hands still enough to get the fire to the end of the cigarette. After a few tries, he gets it lit and stumbles forward across the cobblestones puffing on it and letting hang from his mouth. His white T-shirt and blue jeans hang off his very slight frame. His T-shirt was torn as are the knees of his jeans. He is David Small, Martin Reinders' other boy. As the body disappears on a stretcher into the Catacombs, he sneers and throws the cigarette after it with a flip of his fingers. David walks toward the Catacombs, when one of the cops grabs him by the arm.

"Keeping out of trouble, punk."

David jerks his arm from the policeman's grasp. He pushes his stringy blonde hair off his forehead.

"I'm clean and don't know anything about this and that's all you need to know, pig."

The cop reaches back for his cuffs.

"Good ahead, arrest me. Reinders and his lawyers will have me out again in less than hour."

The cop puts his handcuffs back and turns his back on David and disappears into the darkness. As the cop disappears, David spits after him. Turning he notices, Master and I. Screaming and flailing his arms he yells.

"What the fuck are you looking at?"

David drags himself over and looks me straight in the face. His breath smells of bad whisky.

"Got a problem, boy? You and your pussy Master. Think I killed him. No good son of a bitch. Should have. Maybe I should..."

"If you've got something to say, boy, say it to me," says Master as he steps in front of His slave.

David pulls a bottle of Jack Daniels out of his back pocket and takes a slug.

"I ain't your boy. I belong to the goddamn jerk off that owns this place. Martin fuckin' Reinders. I could have killed that son of a bitch Barry for some of the shit he pulled on me. Will miss him though. He was fun to fuck and push around.

Master looks down at His slave knowing that it is dying to question this "suspect". Master gives it the sign to talk. I cautiously step forward.

"Why could you have killed him?"

"Oh, now the little shit speaks. Because he reneged on some cash and promises he made me."

"For drugs?"

David takes another slug from the whisky bottle and exhales into my face.

"I have no idea what you are talking about."

"But everyone knows you deal..."

David slips the bottle back into his back bottle and clenches his hand trying to decide whether he's going to smash me or not.

"Who told you I deal?"

"That's the worst kept secret since Liberace and Rock Hudson. Everyone knows you deal and use and use too much."

"If that big dumb lummox wasn't standing behind you, could kill you too."

He tries to light another cigarette.

"But I didn't kill him, could have but didn't."

"Why should we believe you?"

David starts to walk around, whirls around.

"Because fuckin' Shershit, you have no fuckin' choice. Don't go poking your nose in my business. What the fuck do you think you are? A pig?"

"No. Curious that's all."

"Well Ellery *Queen*. I just got back. Depending on when old Barry bit it, I was at the liquor store. These shitty bartenders won't give me liquor anymore. Got the receipt here somewhere, n."

David reaches into his pocket, puts out the receipt wads it up and throws it at me. David stumbles over to the opening and turns back."

"Keep your nose clean sub boy or you will not know what happens next when your Master isn't around. Why don't you ask his crummy toady, Jim Lattimer. Now if you two don't mind, I'm tired and getting the fuck away from you."

Master pulls me back to His chest.

David stumbles and falls against the opening's wall. Straightens himself, takes off his shirt showing off his pink skin and continues down into the tunnel.

I bend down and pick up the wad of paper and smooth it out. It read, "Sam's Liquors, one fifth Jack Daniels" and the price. It had a time stamp of 10:02 p.m. Asking Sir the time, he says it is 1:32 p.m. We found the body about midnight I believe. Could David have gotten to the liquor store and back in time to kill Barry? Could he have done it in his condition? God only know what he was on in addition to the liquor.

Master grabs the leash and with one more look around, He leads His slave out of this crime scene.

CHAPTER NINE
BACK INTO THE CATACOMBS

Master and slave round a turn into one of the dark, dank tunnels. At the end of one turn is a lone St. Andrew's cross. It stands out from within the incandescent light at the end of the hall. Master lightly nudges me down the tunnel with the heel of His boot. Feeling my way a long the hard rock wall, I slowly reach the cross. Climbing up on the base of the cross, Sir turns up slightly a small wall light. The yellow light glows behind me as I lower myself on the rack and get comfortable and in position against the cold smooth rigid surface of the wooden cross. Master's hard hands slip my wrists into the thick, black leather restraints and pull them tight and secure. Focus. Need to focus. If David didn't kill him, who would want to kill Barry? Who would have motive for killing him? Would Reinders appear this upset even after knowing he had killed him? Did David get drunk to escape that fact or the fact that he himself killed Barry? The first swing of Sir's flogger cuts through the air with a swoosh and lands with a thud against my back. Focusing on my mind's eye, Master stands shirtless. The hair on his chest sweeps like waving wheat in a field as the wind gently blows over his well-defined pecs and stomach as he stands in the middle of a brightly-lit prairie. He whispers "Come on boy. Come here. Come to me..." repeatedly in a voice tender and strong. The speed and angle of His hits increases. He works the strikes so he can spread the hits from back to my butt and inner thighs. The intensity grows as the thuds give way to the bite of the tips of the tails. My back begins to redden and steam in the cold stillness of the catacombs. The pain is flowing through my body as I can hear Sir's voice is my ears and see him in my closed eyes. Sir's sweat glistens in the sun as it drips over Master's magnificent body. The endorphins kick in and my image of the field becomes murkier and my mind begins to discard the escape as I begin not to feel the cross. The stings keep coming and coming and I welcome the pain as it flows right though me. A goofy smile comes across my face. Not feeling the ground or the cross or the bounds holding me to it, the darkness of the Catacomb begins to swallow me up. I go up on my toes but as quickly I'm back down on the soles of my feet as Master slows down. I flex my back and my skin sticks to itself. The light and the field begins to fade as I drift back. The pain comes rushing back and my body begins to relax. The strikes slow down into thuds. The redness and spotty wounds on my back, butt and thighs are sensitive to the cold. The light from mind fades away as the darkness returns. Slowly Master's rough hands glide lightly over my back slowly fondling what is His. Sir whispers, "Are you there, slave? What are you thinking...feeling?" Can't speak. I melt into the cross as he begins to unhook the restraints. He holds me up with magnificent, furry arm and he releases the other bond. I stand there leaning against the leather, wet hair mixed with his sweat and my manhood responds. He gently kisses my neck.

"Did I tell you slave that you could get a hard-on?"

He gently laughs and leans me up against the cross while he unhooks my feet. Pulling me to him again, he whispers.

"Very good slave. Stand when your ready, 7."

Don't want to stand. I want to lean against Master and be in his arms forever. To feel his touch and melt into him while both of our endorphins explode and meld. Knowing that not only belong to him but the feeling that somehow we are one. It is incredible. Don't want to let it go. But know that I must stand because I must serve His needs not mine. Slowly lifting myself from His chest, this slave tries to regain equilibrium and take my head in my hands. He rubs the back of my neck and slowly kisses it again. Slowly turning and bowing my head, I grateful thank Sir. Reattaching the leash to my neck, I looked back over my shoulder once more at the cross as Master slowly leads us back into the catacombs.

CHAPTER TEN
THE BOY'S BOY

The metal door slams behind us and we make our way into the maze of hallways once again. Master's not tired. That is apparently obvious because of His devilish smile. He pulled me into one of the rows of rooms. Rounding a corner, we see the cleaning cart standing next to an open door, but no one in sight. An assortment of cleaning solvents, brushes, and rags litter the top of the cart with a garage bag hanging off it half full He turns around to me.

"I'm sure they won't mind me fucking you mercilessly as long as I have you clean the room afterwards."

As we approach, I smell the heavy scent of alcohol. But the strange thing is that isn't the scent of rubbing alcohol. A door at the end of the row lies slightly ajar with light streaming out from the cracked door. Master approaches slowly and knocks. No answer. Master takes his flogger from of his hip and uses the handle to slowly push the door open. The first thing we see is a hand slumping by the base of the regularly pale yellow wooden platform. Sir stops and pulls me ahead.

"Slave, I think the mystery deepens."

Sliding the rest of the door open, I peer in. A pair of eyes stares up at me not expressing anything but blankness. The boy is young, I would guess

22 or 23, dressed in a black Anchor T-shirt cut off at the stomach and a pair of tight short jean shorts and barefoot. No doubt about whom it is. The smart-ass kid that checked us in Barry's boy, Jim Lattimer.

He lies slumped forward on the thin mattress of the bathhouse bed. No evidence of violence on the body except for some deep red marks around the throat. A spilled bottle of Jack Daniels sits almost empty in a pool underneath his right hand. Very clearly not breathing. No pulse. Master orders out of the room. Removing the black hanky from his left pocket, he closes the door.

Easy to identify. It was Jim Lattimer.

"Strangled to shut him up, Sir? Why kill him too?"

"That's what I have you to find out, isn't it, slave?"

CHAPTER ELEVEN
THE MAN AND THE MESSAGE

The maze of hallways seems longer than it did, but as this slave has to remain silent, it gives me time to think. First, Barry Wilmot dies. Then his boy, Jim Lattimer. Could Wilmot have told Lattimer something that got him killed? Also, it must have been easy to choke a kid who was already allegedly drunk, or was the liquor taken from the storeroom or the bar so he would be dismissed as drunk, covering up the choking and giving the killer time to get away? Why choke the kid when the weapon for blunt force trauma, which killed Barry, may or may not still be close at hand? Did Latimer try to blackmail the killer? Why he was left may be obvious. The killer had no time to dispose of the body and of course, it can supposed that the reason he didn't come to see the body of his late Sir is that he may have been dead or being killed while I was waiting for Master to return. Of course, Sir and Reinders and the others might have heard him being killed if he was killed around then. Maybe the killer took the opportunity of the noise, loud music and everyone else focused on Barry's body to commit the crime knowing everyone would be distracted. Too many possibilities and not enough facts. Wish I could dust for fingerprints but the cleaning cart was right there all the killer could do was spray wipe and dispose of his towel in the bag with the others. He could then hide or retreat in any room at any time or return to the bar or hide in the catacombs and act like nothing happened.

Just as that thought crossed my mind, I shook myself out of the haze and there he was – the man from the Music Room. Spotting Sir and I, he takes off running. Sir follows after pulling my leash hard and dragging me running behind him to keep up. We chase around hallways and more hallways, but the guy shows no sign of slowing down. The glint of the item in his hand can be seen from time to time. Master drops the leash and it is all I can do to keep up with Sir's powerful legs. As I rush around the corner, I run into Sir smack on. He wavers and looks at me on the floor.

"What are you doing slave? Get up! Now, you see because of your clumsiness, we lost him."

Master turns me over and removing the belt from his waist. "Forty. Count them out loud, slave."

Sir has no build. I take them full force. My ass is bright red and big black marks are apparent. I apologize to Sir. He picks up the leash and we continue to the front and Reinders' office.

On entering the Pit, Master walks up to Master McGuinn and taps him on the shoulder. Master McGuinn was watching a piercing scene taking place in front of him.

"Hello, my friend. What's the rush?"

Master asks for the way to Reinders' office and Master McGuinn offers to show Him. "Have to wait for my replacement to get here. Got to wait for Erskine to get here, ya know." Rob Erskine is the publicity agent for The Anchor but he sometimes helps out around the place. He's rather tall and lanky. His long face shows lines around the eyes and mouth. His blondish hair is fading to a sort of dirty blondish gray.

Master orders me to kneel where I am and He starts to pace.

Master Bill looks back at us. "Is it that important?" Master says that it is and tells him about the finding of the body of Jim Lattimer. Jerry the bootblack enters the Pit from the other way. He puts his hand on Master McGuinn's shoulder and asks if he can work a little longer. Erskine's in the bar.

"He's a mess, Bill. Seems he actually liked the little rat." Jerry smiles. "Oops. I mean, Barry."

Bill tells Jerry that Jim Lattimer has been killed as well and Jerry offers to take us to Reinders' office.

On our way that, Jerry stops, "Don't tell the boss this but Barry may have been his favorite but everyone hated the little shit. The only ones who like him were his boy, Jim and Ron Erskine. Plenty had motive to kill him."

Master asked Jerry if he did.

"You bet your sweet ass I could have. So could have Tim. So could have all the bartenders and bar backs. He was massive prick. Barry used to play games with the tip jars. We know what we took in and we know what he gave us. I think he was siphoning some of it for himself. The louse. Tim and I work very hard. Reinders. He did nothing about it. Supposed our tips won't be a problem tonight."

Jerry leaves us at the office and without a word, turning quickly on his heals, he scurries away as Master turns the knob.

"7. Don't you have any idea who is doing this?"

Master does not open the door.

"Beginning to understand Sir but need to know more, Sir. We will know when we know why they died."

Grunting at my crypticness, Sir knocks and voice bellows from the other side:

"Come in already!"

CHAPTER TWELVE
FATHER OF THE CORPSE

Reinders' large office is decorated but chaotic. Framed Mr. World Leatherman posters, pictures of his leather family, plaques, awards, and original art line almost every inch of the walls that is not occupied by dozens of shelves. These shelves, actually almost every inch of surface is piled with file boxes, papers, pamphlets, and books. Across the front edge of the desk is a long black leather flogger. Its handle reads "Mr. World Leatherman – Da Boss" in small metal studs. Reinders sits behind his desk looking sullen and tired. For a man who usually doesn't look or act like his advanced age, he looks every bit of it and more.

Master informs Reinders about what he has just found. While he is doing so, the brunette lady sweeps into the office. Getting a better look at her, I can see she is wearing a black blouse unbuttoned to show a black lace bra, a denim skirt and short basic black low-heeled shoes.

Reinders rubs his face with his hands.

"This is my assistant, Diane Cofile. Been with me for years. Diane, let's get the cops back here. Now Jerry's dead too."

Without emotion, Diane walks over to a smaller desk in the far corner of the room, presumably hers, and picks up the receiver and dials.

Master takes a seat in a padded black leatherette seat in front of Reinders' desk and orders me to kneel at His right.

"How are you, Sir?" inquires Master.

"How am I? How am I? Barry's dead. Jim's dead. My family is dying. The cops keep coming here. Do you know what this will do for my business? I lost my boy and then lost his boy and maybe my business in one crazy. How the hell am I supposed to feel?"

Reinders sighs and takes a swig from the coffee cup on his desk.

"Yeah, I knew Barry was cheating on me. Somehow having Jim. It wasn't enough. I didn't care. He is...was young. Thought let him sow some wild oats. At his age, kids will be a little wild. God knows I was. It was the lying about the cheating that killed me. If he had just been honest with me."

Forgetting myself, I asked him how he found out that Barry was cheating. Master allowed it.

"Was walking down to the pop machine and heard him speaking. The music in the hallway drowned out parts but I got enough to figure out he was talking to his paramour, I guess. Decided not to interrupt. Would handle it at home. Better to handle it at home. But, that night, I didn't discuss it. Not that night or the next.

Doesn't make any difference now."

Master asks him who he would think would want Barry and Lattimer dead.

"Don't know. Wish I did. As bad as it sounds I know one person who is glad Barry's dead. He just left my office. Larry Sheldrake. He owns the bar Clark's up the street. The one that burned. He's got some crazy notion that since he thinks Barry burned his bar and I should pay to rebuild it.

Seems the insurance doesn't cover all the damage. I didn't even know Barry had offered to buy it from him. Barry and I discussed him having his own place someday but didn't think he meant this soon."

Reinders explains that Sheldrake said the fire started when some alcohol in the back room ignited and exploded unintentionally; engulfing, Daddy Don's boy, Greg, that had come in early to do inventory.

"Sheldrake blamed Barry because he refused to sell him the bar. I told him to tell his staff to stop smoking in the storeroom.

Poor Greg. He was nice kid. Larry wanted to know what I was going to do about it."

"What did you say?" I asked.

"Is he supposed to talk?" Master gave me a light corrective tap to my head. He didn't disapprove of me asking questions under these circumstances, but I guess he was hoping Reinders would continue.

"Nothing. He has no proof other than customers and staff saw Barry hanging around the bar on the day of the fire. Still Larry says that alcohol was used as an accelerate to start the fire or so the cops and fire department told him it was. But if Larry did kill them, I'll be damned to how he died."

Master smacks me on the head to get my attention away from being riveted on Reinders.

"Speak, slave. My slave is good at puzzles, Mr. Reinders. Well, any thoughts or conclusions, boy?"

Both Master and Martin Reinders are glaring at me.

"Mr. Reinders, I think I can piece enough together, Sirs, to make some sense. We know when Barry died. Sometime between 10 and midnight.

By my best guess, Jim Lattimer, died just before, because he didn't come when his Sir, Barry, was killed. He also wasn't killed the same way. The weapon used on Barry was probably a flash idea bred out of convenience."

Reinders takes two Arthritis Strength Excedrin from a bottle in his top desk drawer and washes it down from a bottle of water on his desk.

The door swings open and Tim, pokes his head in. The police are here again the police sergeant wants to talk to Reinders. He gets out of his chair slowly. It is very noticeable that this whole evening is taking quiet a toll on him and aging him quickly. Reinders shows Master and I out and I look back as Reinders returns to his desk and Diane shows the officer in and closes the door.

CHAPTER THIRTEEN
GOING HOME?

Master walks over to the bar and orders a beer. I kneel at His boots. Master orders me to stand. He puts a bottle of water in front of me. Jerry starts to close down his stand for the night. The first time I can really look around the bar. Erskine is sitting on the corner of the bar. He slowly sipping on a cup of black coffee he keeps cupped in both hands. Tim is wiping down the bar with a bar rag. He tosses the cap from my water on the ground behind the bar. His bright smile has been downgraded to a smirk. Master takes a gulp of His beer. The foam lingers on His bushy mustache until He licks it off. At the other end of the bar is Daddy Don. He has leaned his head on the hand and is snoring lightly. The paramedics come through behind us with the stretcher with the body of Jim Lattimer. Master unclips the flogger from His waist and plops it on the bar. Stretching, Master Bill comes into the bar and up to us.

"The damn cops shut the Pit down to look for evidence." Tim plops an ale in front of him. "Plus I have to send my new boy home. This sucks." Master Bill takes two large gulps and pulls up a stool. Bill starts to tell Sir about a skinny kid who came up to service him while he was watching The Pit.

CHAPTER FOURTEEN
THE OTHER BOY

Over my shoulder, I see him again. The mysterious man is there again. It gleams again in His hand. Jerking at Sir's shirt, Sir brushes away my hand. Master Bill is still talking about the kid.

"He had the sucking of a vacuum cleaner. Felt like my cock was going to get pulled off my body."

On my second look back, he recognizes Sir and I start to back away from the entrance to the bar. I pull harder on Sir's shirt. The man turns and started to run.

"Sorry Sir," I yell as I leave His side, but I couldn't let him get away again.

Speeding up, I find him around the corner.

As I round the corner in pursuit of him, a hand reaches out and firmly grasps my shoulder spinning me around and slamming me up against a door. The door isn't locked and I sprawl flat on my ass flat in the middle of the small play room.

I look up into the enraged face of Sir who screams at me to stay put or he'll "punish me more than I am already getting."

"But he's getting away, Sir. The man with the knife. "All angers leaves his face and he pulls me back to my feet and we continue the chase.

A few minutes later Sir shoves the man in to a bathhouse room. The mysterious man is very noticeably shaken and very desperate to get away. Sir blocks the doorway with his large massive frame.

"Go ahead speak Holmes, but watch your step, boy," Sir demands.

The man, who turn out to be very slight of frame underneath his large coat. He stands about a foot and half shorter than Sir. Besides the coat he I wearing a simple black pocket shirt, a pair of blue jeans and black sneakers. He shook as he awaits my questions.

"Wha...What do you want with me?"

I look up at Sir and he makes a motion with His hand to get on with it.

"Your name for starters."

"Norman Belgrove. Who are you?"

From the doorway, Master bellows that it doesn't matter who I am. "I own him. Ask your next questions, boy!"

"What are you doing here?"

"Trying to find a way to Reinders and then a way out of here before I get killed, but now the cops won't let anyone leave."

He played with the object in his hand. I walk over and open His hand. It is a silver cigarette lighter.

"I like to play with it when I am nervous and scared."

"What do you have to be scared of?"

"Like how the two of you are going to kill me like you killed Sir or how you killed poor Jim."

After we assured him that we were not the killers, the whole story came out.

"I guess it was me who Mr. Reinders heard with Sir. I loved Barry Wilmot. Was auditioning to become His second boy after Jim Lattimer, of course. Jim was going to be my big brother. I saw Barry last just outside the door to the Pit and we were going to meet there later to play a little after Master McGuinn was off shift. For some reason Master McGuinn doesn't like Barry much. Even yelled at him to kiss his ass and threatened to kill Barry once. Or so Sir told me."

It was all there. He had met Barry in secret to see if they really liked each other and then a couple dates, if he worked out and made progress as a boy, Barry was going to tell Reinders.

"I was sticking around hoping Sir had a free moment to spend with me. It was very demanding of him to run this place. We used to meet just outside the Catacombs and there I was waiting in the shadows by the big door when I saw Sir. Ron Erskine was running after him. It was obvious they had been fighting and Sir didn't want to hear anymore of it. He marched into the Catacombs slamming that big door in the face of Ron. After Ron had grumbled and walked away, I opened the door and quietly went inside. I ashamed to admit but I lost him in the Catacombs. The next time I saw him, his body was being carried out. Sir's dead. Jim's dead. Can't you see I'm next?"

Somehow I managed to get him calmed down, but still not totally convinced that he wasn't third in line.

"You see who ever the killer is he got rid of our Sir and his main boy. Reinders is too big and careful so I'm next."

Out of the blue I decided to ask him about the fire at Clark's.

"Greg was never meant to die. He wasn't even meant to be involved. Greg wasn't even supposed to be there. We got in before the bar was even schedule to open. Sir had a spare key made and told me to let myself in, go to the back storage room and to set the sterno cans near under a can of open beer. It would explode and cause a tremendous explosion and a big mess. That's all it was supposed to cause, a big mess."

Norman's begins to panic and I reach out to hold him by his arms. Tears fall from His eyes and his breathing labors.

"I...I... I didn't mean... what I mean to say is...I didn't mean for Greg to get hurt or the bar to burn. It was a prank. A stupid prank because that Sheldrake guy wouldn't sell Sir the bar. He wanted to show Mr. Reinders that he could do more. Be worth more. But heldrake wouldn't sell. So Sir sent me to this stupid prank."

Norman rested his head and started to sob even heavier.

"No one is blaming you, Norman. Sure if the police knew..."

Norman pulls away from me and runs right up to Sir who stands still. Twisting back, he shows me his panic stricken face.

"But you can't tell them. They'll put me away. For a long time. For years. For eternity."

At this point, amused by the way things have progressed, Master calmly says that we boys need to be calm and head back to the bar.

Norman walks past him to the hallway. "You, stay boy. Hide until we come and get you. You'll be safer from behind a locked door."

Norman answers "Yes, Sir."

Sir gets right up in my face. "Well, slave...Do you solve this, now or do I beat you with my flogger within an inch of your life for running away the way you did."

"That's it! I know how it was done, and I know how to find out who did it."

"Because of I threatened to beat you?"

"No Sir. Sir can we please see Martin Reinders., now?"

CHAPTER FIFTEEN
THE TEST

They were all still sitting around the bar. Master talked the police to keep these folks around a little longer. Sure he thought he was screwy but since, he confided, he was no further along in knowing for himself that he would take a chance and give the slave a chance

I fetch Norman to the bar. Erskine and Master Bill are still sitting there. Bill looks unhappy but a little toasty.

Jerry stands next to chair and smiling folds his bootblack shoe shine rags from the evening and starting to put them away.

Reinders and his assistant, Diane, come out of the office. A cop escorts Daddy Don back into the bar explain that he caught him trying to get His coat.

"I was cold. I'm an old man you know," he protests. Also police escort into the room, a tallish heavyset man with a bushy mustache, the owner of Clark's, Larry Sheldrake.

"This is no way to treat me, guys. Guys. I used to be a cop. Why would I break the law now? Let me go. Guys."

Last to join us is Reinders' other boy, David. An officer reports the

Superintendent that they found "the little freak in one of the rooms, hypodermic on the floor next to him." He presents the needle in an evidence bag next to him. Reinders grabs David in the arm and orders him to take a seat at the bar.

Daddy Don unclips his flogger from his belt and grabs a seat at the bar. Reinders orders beers all around and Tim takes the orders.

As a slave, I am happier when it is all about Sir but Master shoves me out into the middle of the room and makes sure I live up to His word.

The bar is never this crowded and this silent. The only sound seems to be my heart beating in my chest. Can Master hear it? Can they all hear it? I take a deep breath.

"Thank You Sirs and Ma'am."

I lick my lips and take another deep breath. Tim offers me a glass of water. I refuse.

"This just one humble slave's attempt and I do not mean to offend or disrespect anyone..."

Erskine whines, "Great. This is going to be solved by some shitty slave." Master glares at him.

"Get on with it," yells Martin Reinders.

One last deep breath.

"Fine. Barry was killed between 10 and midnight. According to the coroner, he was killed by blunt force trauma to the back of the head with a rounded instrument."

The police superintendent concurs. "He was killed by a rounded instrument that had to have some weight to it and very little indention or grooving. We looked but could not find a screwdriver or lead pipe that matched the wound."

This slave continues. "I think some time after or sometime before, Jim Lattimer was strangled, perhaps to shut him up for whatever else he knew or was into with Barry. It makes sense it was before because he did not come running when his Sir's, Barry's body was discovered."

David picks up his limp head. His eyes are bloodshot. "Son of bitch helped me with the drugs. Took a cut for himself tonight. Killer got the money."

An officer walks up behind David. Reinders doesn't protest.

Jerry pipes up. "Maybe he knew about Barry skimming our tips."

"But Jerry Sir, would that be enough of a reason to kill them Both?"

"We'll there was the stuff with Clark's next door," suggests Diane.

But before Sheldrake can protest, Norman burst off from his spot in the corner, crying out. "I didn't mean to do it. I did what Barry told me. It was a prank. Only a prank."

Norman falls to his knees crying. The veins in Sheldrake's neck throb. He is too angry to speak.

"I think I know who did it and how to prove it"

I ask Tim for the first aid kid hidden behind the bar and a roll of paper towels.

"Sir's may I see your floggers?"

Daddy Don whois still groggy asks, "You want to see my what, boy?"

But Martin Reinders doesn't hestitate.

"I'll see this silliness," says Martin Reinders retrieves his special one off his desk. Soon I have everyone else's as well including Master's.

Slurring, David yells, "Well Ellery Queen, get on with it!"

I set each flogger on its own individual paper towel.

"We know that the weapon had a rounded surface and we know it was carried away as easily as it was brought. It was something Master said that made me think. Floggers have weighted handles. Many times they are weighted with shot, wood, or some kind of metal to counter weight it in the hand. What if the murderer in a flash grabbed for their flogger to strike him with and wielded it like the police wield a truncheon. When I was cleaning to clean Master's leather, I learned that you can never entirely get blood out of leather. If there is any left, peroxide will react with it."

Opening the first aid kit, I remove the bottle of Hydrogen Peroxide. Master Bill's, Daddy Don's, Sir's and Martin Reinders's foggers all sit one next to the other. I grab the package of individual cloth bandages. I wipe alcohol on Master Bill's. No reaction. I know I am on the right track... Sir's flogger. No reaction. No surprise there. Daddy Don's. Hesitantly, I wipe. No reaction. Reasonably really. he would have been too drunk at the time to strike with any real force. If this doesn't have a reaction, If this doesn't work Master will punish me for months, maybe years. Alcohol. Wipe. Reaction. Incredulously, I turn back to all of them and hold up Martin Reinders' flogger. He turns stark white.

"I loved Barry. I still love Barry. Why would I kill him? How did mine have the blood. Nobody has access to that office other than Diane and I. I keep it locked all times. Besides I couldn't do it.".

"That's right, Sir. I saw you take medication for arthritis before you left the room to meet with the police."

"I have arthritis bad in both hands. Comes with being my age."

"And makes it impossible for you to strike the blow"

The slave walks behind Reinders. "That leaves you, Diane."

"You have no proof and no motive."

"I noticed it when we were in the office before. You do well hiding your weight, but it is not that you like desserts, is it? How many months?"

Diane finally cracks a smile. "7 and it's a boy."

"And Barry's the father, right? What happened? He wouldn't pay for the abortion? Didn't want to support the kid?"

"We didn't need his support. The child is for me and my lover, Lori. We are going to raise it. The child won't need a father."

"If you got what you wanted then why double homicide? What could Barry do to effect the outcome of this child? Was it his sperm?"

Diane grabs Erskine's coffee cup out of his hand and nearly misses the slave.

"That's it. Wasn't he the sperm donor?"

"You...you..."

"Did he give you Lattimer's sperm instead and represented it as his own?"

"You son of bitch," she screams. "How did you? How can you? Yes. Lattimer was a no-good drunken weasel of a kid. Barry told me he would do it, but he switched it. He switched it on me. He told me last night. He laughed and thought it was funny. He laughed in my face. I couldn't let him get away with it. Think I'm going to have a child of drunken imbecile."

Jerry shouts, "Could be worse. David could be the father."

David scowls, spits at him and falls flat on his face trying to get off the stool. The officer helps him up rewarding with a pair of shiny bracelets while one his fellow officers Mirandizes Diane.

CHAPTER SIXTEEN
THE NEXT WEDNESDAY

The next Wednesday, *Windy City Times* had a front page story on how the Police Superintendent was brilliant and instrumental on solving the case. I cut it out and asked Sir to frame it. He put it in a cheap frame and hung it in His den. Master is proud of me even though he asked the police not to mention either of our names in connection with the case. Master does like his life simple and private.

I put the latest mystery im reading, the latest John Grisham, back on my little reading shelf in the den. Entering the bedroom, Sir isn't in bed. He standing there wide-awake and shirtless except for his leather vest showing off his muscular chest and hard abs in all its furry glory. He has on His Wescos, black leather chaps and leather jock strap. The outline of His engorged member is unmistakable in the pouch. He hits his hand with the business end of a leather crop.

"Hope your butt's clean, slave. I'm going to fuck you long and hard tonight following a good hard beating. You did a good job finding that killer. Deserve to be used and used hard. Come here, slave."

CHAPTER SEVENTEEN
MASTER SPEAKS

He even had to tell about that. Yeah, my slave did a good job. Hard to believe that I am as magnificent as he said I am. All that jazz about "His massive right arm, bristling with black curly fur and taut musculature". But I have better things to do than argue with a slave.

Seems he learned something from all the mysteries he reads. Maybe I'll send him to detective school. Maybe not. I don't know that I want him doing this all the time. Take too much time away form clean house, cooking meal, and servicing me.

Yet, he caught a murderer and Reinders did reward us both with lifetime memberships to The Anchor and VIP status. He also threw in a couple packages to next year's Mr. World Leatherman Contest Weekend and wanted to know if we would head up the security team. Not sure I want to tie up time like that. Not sure I want my own bloodhound or share him as a community bloodhound, even if he is cute occasionally eating out of a dog dish. Will have to think about all this.

Meanwhile, I'm going to drag his ass down to the bedroom. It is always fun fucking, flogging, beating and using him. But then that's what he is for. Dinner was good tonight. Please excuse me. Going to get a little dessert. He is a good slave. Most of the time.

DICK STRONG AND THE CASE OF THE MISSING SLAVE

He came through the door with an air of superiority. The black leather German officer's coat and jodhpurs traced the mighty frame hidden underneath. His thigh high boots shined at me from the doorway but were not bright enough to blind me from the handle of a leather crop hidden in his left boot. He strode up to my desk and took a cigar the size of small table leg from his clenched teeth. Exhaling in my face, he spoke.

"Are you Dick Strong?"

I was disappointed to not hear any attempt at a German accent. Instead it was the guttural speech of an animal of the Bronx. From the looks of all this dead cow in front of me, this one had obviously done well.

"I'm talking to you. Are you Dick Strong?"

"Tops aren't usually concerned about that."

"Don't waste my time."

It was meant as a threat, but I'm not so easily intimidated.

"I'm Master Brutus. I need you to find me a slave."

"Usually all guys like you have to do is flex and you can have fifty."

He left that go by as he reached into the inner coat pocket briefly revealing a mass of thick chest hair. He was a Neanderthal man dressed in black leather. This client was getting more interesting all the time.

"Not just any slave. This one."

The picture was of not just a musclecub but a double musclecub. He had muscles on top of muscles and like his Master he was covered in a thick matte of fur except for his balls and cock which while even inside of a cock cage you could tell were shaved clean. He was looking at the camera from inside a thick steel cage, large Master lock around his neck, and with a very sorry puppy look in his big blue eyes.

I handed the picture back. He motioned me to keep it.

"Never have I seen a slave so secure."

"Still he's gone. Cage and all. I went to bed, locked him in for the night and that was the last I saw of him."

"Where is this picture taken?"

"My garage is my dungeon. It's okay. I made sure it was heated and winterized before I turned it into my slave quarters. It's got floor heat and central a/c."

"What if he needed you?" "He had a panic button in the cage. It buzzes in the main house. There are bells throughout including right by the bed next to my head."

"When did he vanish?"

"Last night."

"And the bell sounded."

"No."

"No?"

"Went to release him for his morning duties and it was gone. I want you to come to the garage and investigate."

"The cops –"

"No cops."

"Why not?"

"Because it will get out. I don't need the other Sirs laughin' at me. Lost a slave, did ya? Embarrassing."

"I get $250 a day plus expenses."

"That much?"

"You want your slave back?"

"Yeah."

"So you can save face?"

"That and for the first time in almost three years I had to use the bowl to piss in. Hate dirtying a perfectly good toilet. Who's going to clean that?"

Heartwarming. He flipped me a Visa and I pulled my boy out from under the desk. Got to keep boys busy or they just get in trouble.

As my boy emerged, his eyes popped.

"How long he'd been down there?"

The boy's body glimmered in the lights coming from the window behind. He was sweaty from the work he was doing. He is lightly covered in blond hair and his long blonde hair hangs down to his shoulders. He's only 22, but he's a fast learner. The boy wears nothing but a thong and kneepads and I prefer it that way.

"No need to worry. He keeps his mouth shut. Actually when he's down there, his mouth is more than occupied."

The boy runs the card and hands me the card and both copies. Then he crawls back under the desk. Nice when you don't have to tell them their place.

The Neanderthal was impressed.

"My pig does that but not as much I would like."

"When can I come out to see the garage?"

"We can go right now, but..."

"He'll do what he's told."

I knock on the desk. "Pull the car around."

Without a sound, the boy, his name is Jason, pulls his clothes on from a bottom desk drawer, and grabs the keys from the top one and heads toward the door.

"Jason, have you forgotten something?"

The boy stops. He pivots and returns to the desk. Kneeling he kisses my crotch, tucks me away, and zips my fly.

"Go get the car."

Jason disappears without another word.

The garage was bigger than I expected and extremely well stocked. A St. Andrews cross, a couple floating tables, a sling, even a clean out station for touch ups. In the middle of floor, a large gaping hole where you could see something had been. Splinters of wood and metal litter the place. The garage door had been all boarded over. Now parts of it were only good for kindling. I had propped Jason in the corner where I could watch him salivate. I knew what was on his mind. He was imaging the uses we could do with all this equipment. Somehow it seemed wrong to want to beat and fuck your boy in the middle of a crime scene.

"It was over 1000 pounds," the Neanderthal said.

"Big boy."

"I meant the cage. It was wrought iron with a deep matte black finish."

"And the slave was in it?"

"Yeah."

"And the slave's name?"

"Does it matter?"

"Sometimes. It might help."

"His birth name is James Dutton. We don't use that no more."

"And now?"

"Caesar."

"Because he is a king among slaves or because Brutus killed Caesar?"

"The second. He wants to be showed who's boss."

"They crashed through that door."

"They?"

"Obvious there had been more than one of them. Caesar was in his cage?"

"All locked away for the night. I had catheterized him in case he needed to piss during the night. The plug was up his ass. I had lube it up a lot more."

"Why is that?"

"His ass was extra sore last night. I felt like it, okay?"

"Don't have to ask me. He's your slave."

"Damn right."

A scan of the grounds outside added no new information. This makes no sense. If the slave was the target, why take the cage? Why not just cut the lock?

I got back to the office and dictated to Jason the facts, as I knew them which so far wasn't much. Then he was going to go back to his usual position, but the phone rang. It was Lieutenant Samuels. Don't like him sucking my dick while the Lieutenant is on the phone. Always makes me feel like somehow he knows and wants him for under his desk.

"Where's your secretary, Strong? Been trying to get you all day."

"Had to let him go. His friends caught him doing something he shouldn't have."

"Anything I should know about?"

No, but his friends weren't happy. They ruined a perfectly good pair of Prada shoes by pouring cement all over them. Uptown let me know."

"Sorry, kid. Too bad about the secretary and the shoes. We found something I think that is right up your alley."

They had found a large metal cage in the weeds off the river.

"Is that all?"

"Yeah. The crime scene techs say the guy whoever he was had been plugged up front and back. They found a bag of piss and..."

I could hear the paper rattle as he consulted his notepad.

"A large flesh colored silicon object that he subtle specks of feces and was covered in a substance made with Nonoxynol-9. It was pyramid shaped."

"It's called a butt plug."

"You would know that. From the looks of the thing, you never get anything that size up my butt."

"You were always a tightass, Samuels."

"Hey. I'm doing you a favor calling you at all."

"Any sign of a body?"

There hadn't been. It had taken ten officers and a tow truck to even get the cage to budge from its muddy location. If you were going to go to that much trouble, why not at least sell the damn thing for scrap. Maybe they're selling the object inside. I had heard about the market in trained leather slaves. Something like Caesar might go for a high commodity even if he wasn't trained for things like secretarial, gardening, housework, cooking, or home maintenance.

I made a few phone calls. One scrap peddler had described a group of six guys who had tried to sell a black wrought iron cage. There had been a seventh guy but as he said, "It was almost like he wasn't allowed out of the car.

"It smelled fishy, yah know so I turned them down." In addition to the car, a white Ford Escort, they had had a Dodge Ram truck. The cage was on the back of that. He didn't have a good description other they had tight shirts and jeans, boots on their feet and all looked like powerful muscular men.

"They were the kind that could give serious hurt if they wanted to."

I went home and Jason had dinner on the table. His ass was dessert. No matter how hard I bang, he always presses back for more. Hungriest hole I have ever known. I left a couple good loads all over his pretty face and then kicked him along to go get my leathers Bootblack Marc was nothing but predictable sometimes. His mouth on the well licked boots of a hot top begging to get further up his leg. Not this time. The Sir complemented him on his good job, padded his head and tossed him a twenty. I climbed into the chair.

He bent over to lick my boots but I pulled his head back up. He looked genuinely disappointed.

"Only information tonight?"

"Yeah. There's a C in it for you."

"More then I'm going to make tonight. Smell a Cock is dead so far."

"What do you know about a Master Brutus."

"And slave Caesar?"

"Yes, boy."

"Caesar's a good sort. Smart too. Talked to him for a long time at the last MAsT gathering."

"And the Sir?"

"Caesar's devoted to him but Brutus is basically as dumb as a box of rocks. Knows his way around a dungeon though and has a big beer can of a cock that Caesar likes a lot."

"Anything else I should know? What do the other Masters think?"

"They think Brutus is a joke and Caesar is too good for him."

"Got that on good authority?"

"Yeah, well, slaves talk."

"Get to work on my boots. We don't too bore yours."

Master George was in his usual place across the bar where he could watch his boy get his job done."

Marc pulls out the Lexol and starts to work.

"Find him yet?"

"You know?"

"Everyone does."

"Brutus didn't want it getting out."

"Too late."

"So who are these guys?"

I dangled the C note between my legs and let it slip up the outline of my cock in the black leather. He noticed.

"All I can tell you is he is being taught a lesson."

"By whom?"

"A bunch of Masters. They want to take Brutus down a peg."

"Why?"

"He keeps trying to show them up. That and he has an ego a size to dwarf the Goodyear blimp."

"And Caesar?"

"I don't know where he is. Sure he is fine."

"How do I find these guys?"

"I don't. They contact Sir and off we go."

"So I'll go talk to your Sir."

Fear showed in his eyes and he begged me not to.

"He doesn't know anymore than I and he'd kill me if we never went to another their parties."

"Hot?"

"That's an understatement."

"So far I don't think this worth a C-note."

"Fine. Go to Jake's Gym. He'll know how you can find them."

Bootblack Marc hadn't steered me wrong...so far.

Jake was shutting the placer for the night when the boy and I arrived.

Jake had ripped off his shirt showing a body any wrestler would be proud of with large pecs, six packs matted with fur and tattoos.

"I think I know the guys you mentioned. They have a private dungeon on the South Side. Not the safest neighborhood but when those neighbors hear screams they are less likely to ask questions."

Jake had to go clean the steam room. Before he did we messed it up a little more. Two muscular tops and one willing bottom with two holes and no waiting. The boy was up for it all. Even when we tied him to one of the machines and body punched him; he took it like a champ. By the end of it, his ass was bright red, bruises all over, a sore jaw and butthole and a big smile on his face. He gulped the last half-liter of my piss before we showered and bid Jake adieu address to the dungeon in my back pocket.

Jason stayed in the car with the doors locked while I went in. I hung against the walls as I crept my way into the building. The door was open almost like they had expected me, but I was taking no chances. It had been a large warehouse, but now it was broken into long hallways full of offices. All was particleboard and barrenness. The only sound was my own breathing and heart beat. Around a couple more corners was a bright light and finally voices.

"Where is he?" one voice asked.

"Caesar. Got him tied up on the web. Beat his cock with the large paddle until he came. He's happier than a pig in slop."

"No, that meddling detective. Jake said he was on his way. His car is in front."

"Cute boy in it too."

The element of surprise was gone. So I walked into the room. After all, I was expected.

"Hello, gents. Dick Strong, meddling detective and you are?"

"Masters Ronanelli and Martins."

"Let's cut to the chase. I've come to take Caesar home."

"Can't let you do that?"

When big musclemen start telling me I can't do something it usually doesn't turn out well.

"Why not?"

"Because we don't want him there."

"Let me see him."

"He's fine," Master Martins growls.

"Mind if I judge for myself."

"Yes."

Knew they weren't going to make this easy.

Another muscleman enters the room. Shirtless his wavy blonde hair matched the ringlets off his chest and abs.

"Mr. Strong, please excuse the rudeness of my club brothers. They are not exactly admirers of Master Brutus. I'm Master Simpson."

Master Ronanelli spins around to Simpson. "Brutus' a schmuck."

"I'd like to see Caesar."

"Certainly, Mr. Strong. We can let you see him, but he stays."

"His Master sent me to bring him home."

Without a word Master Simpson led down a flight of stairs and into a large back room. A huge well stock dungeon for any scene possible met my eyes. My cock stiffens slightly at the thought of what I had in the car and what I could do with him here.

They took to me to a large inside room. We turned the corner and there were three more musclemen and two boys. Caesar was tied to a cross getting beaten on my two of these guys and the other had my boy, Jason, by the arm. Jason is thrown at my feet.

"You should protect what is your better than just locking it in a car." Jason quickly crawls behind me hiding in back of my legs. From his hand on my thigh, I feel him shake. "He's very young but seems very dependent."

"I came here to find Caesar not to have boy judged."

A loud moan comes followed by a large crack. It turn around toward the noise. Jason follows one step behind me not letting me go. Caesar is naked and tied to a cross. Master Ronanin is hitting him a single tail.

Master Simpson stops beside me. "See told you Caesar was happy. He will go home eventually. When we are done."

So that was their plan. Use and abuse Caesar. Play to all his kinks, fantasies, and sexual proclivities. Then send him home to Brutus. Show Caesar he doesn't measure up. They get revenge on a pompous ass and a great slave running to be back with them. What could be better?

Master Ronanelli cleans up Caesar's back and then releases the restraints and lets him fall back into his arms. I walk up. Caesar was clearly flying.

In the end and once he came down, Caesar agree to go back to Master Brutus', but they had one their job too well.

At the next MasT meeting, Caesar was at Master Simpson's feet. I saw Master Brutus later at the bar skulking in the shadows.

As for Jason, I installed eyehooks in the car so he couldn't be dragged from it so easily again.

Afterwards, I took him home and beat his ass black and blue and then rode him hard. He smiled afterwards and kissed my feet before curling up in my arms to sleep. Good to have a boy who does what he is told.

REDNECK FANTASY

Pedro wakes up in a gray cement room. Water drips off the pipes. The room is empty except for him and the chair he is tied into. He struggles against the ropes, but he is tied securely to the wooden chair. Even his ankles are tied to the legs of the chair. He struggles more but all he can feel is the ropes tightening and biting into his naked flesh.

The door behind him flies open and is slammed closed again with a loud clap. Two men with biceps bulging from under sleeveless flannel shirts, tight 501s and big Carolina work boots circle the tied man. Charlie spits the chew from his mouth on to the floor.

"Hey look Clyde. A spic and he's all ours."

"Let's string him up. Kill the cacaroach."

"We will," says Charlie. "We will but first let's have some fun with him." He laughs.

Charlie leans down into Pedro's face. "Yup. We'll torture this one a good long time."

Pedro continues to struggle. "You understand no Englisho?"

He glares back at Charlie.

"No hablo English?"

"I understand."

Clyde walks closer. "Look. It can talk."

"I'm not an it. My name is Pablo."

"Oooo Pablo." Charlie back hands him across the face. "You're name is what ever I say it is, spic boy. I'll make you sorry you ever come here from Mehico."

"Honduras."

"What did you say, boy?" Charlie demands.

"My family is Honduran."

"It don't matter. It's all Mexico to me."

Clyde walks up and spits in his face. Charlie puts his leg up on the chair and drives his heel into Pablo's balls.

"It don't matter where the fuck you come from, because we're going to fuck you up so bad yo mama won't recognize you."

He digs his heel in deeper and the scream that Pablo was stifling fills the room.

Both rednecks lean back and laugh.

Charlie goes around and kicks the chair forward. Pedro lands on his front with a thump. Clyde checks.

"He's conscious."

"Good. Hold his head. I want him to feel it all."

Clyde holds Pablo head. Charlie rips the belt from its loops and holding both ends brings it crashing down on Pablo's ass.

Pablo screams. Clyde whispers, "Scream as much as you want. There's no one to hear."

Each stoke the belt comes down harder and harder. Pablo tries to catch his breath but the assault is relentless.

Charlie laughs as he sees Pablo's ass get redder and redder. Every time he brings his hand down he can feel more and more heat off the smooth skin.

"Stop. Please stop," Pablo cries.

"No hablo English," Charlie screams as he goes for one more swat.

Charlie keeps swinging until Pablo's ass is bright red.

Clyde looks up bored. "Is that all you are going to do is beat this spic's ass?"

Charlie throws the belt aside. "We'll what do you want me to do?"

Clyde lays Pablo on his side. Standing up he un-buttons his fly.

"What you doing, Clyde?"

"I'm going to remind him of the Rio Grande. He likes water. I'm going to give him some."

Clyde pulls out his beer can size dick and releases a stream of golden piss on Pablo's head.

Pablo closes his eyes but taste the sweet almondy taste on his lips.

"We'll since you've gone and got your dick out..."

Charlie takes a bottle lube, a condom, and a knife out of his pocket and then lets his pants drop. His large uncut cock is at full attention.

He flicks the knife open right in front of Pablo. Pablo tries to jump up but Charlie has his knee in the middle of his back. Charlie cuts the bonds the hold Pablo to the chair. He flicks the knife closed and slips the protection on, he lubes up his cock and rams it as hard as he can in Pablo's red ass. Pablo's scream bounces off the walls as his butt hole is ripped open by the sudden thrust. Charlie rids his ass hard like a cowboy breaking in a new bronco. Clyde cheers him on as Charlie continues to ride Pablo as hard as he wants.

Flipping Pablo on his back, he throws Pablo's feet in the arm and continues the ass assault. Clyde bends down and grabs hold of Pablo's nips twisting and digging into them with his nails.

Charlie huffs, "Don't twist them. Hit them."

Clyde pulls his hands off Pablo's nips and starts to pec punch him mercilessly. Pablo doesn't know where to react. The fucking is feeling great but hard as heck and now they are beating on him again. "Deal with the pain. Deal with it and they may keep you alive," he thinks to himself.

Clyde's pec punching is almost rhythmic as Charlie's fucking is hard, sloppy and deep.

Pablo's cock starts to dribble. Charlie pulls out and shoots a large load all over Pablo.

"Man, if you were going to cum, you could have warned me."

"Sorry Clyde."

Clyde rips off his shirt exposing smooth chest and six pack. He wipes himself off.

"Take that spic boy." And Charlie spit on him again.

Pablo lies still.

"My turn."

Charlie tosses Clyde a condom and the bottle of lube. "Ride 'em, cowboy. See if you can loosen up that tight hole."

Clyde rolls it on, lubes up and he's in riding as hard as Charlie was before.

"Nice hole."

Charlie kicks Pablo a few times then bends down and resumes the pec punching. Pablo already has red and black bruises on his chest.

Clyde's making animal noises with each thrust. It is not long before he too stands up.

"Get back Charlie."

Charlie jumps out of the way as Clyde releases a massive shower of cum all over Pablo. Pablo reaches for himself but Clyde kicks his arm out the way.

"You ain't going to die with a smile on your face."

Pablo stumbles to his feet and Charlie grabs his arms and pulls them back. Clyde continues the pummeling except this time it is on stomach as well.

"Please. I'll give you anything. Stop."

"Here that, Clyde, he thinks he can come to our country and tell us what to do."

"I'm...I'm an American. I was born here."

"Hear that lie. Hit 'em harder."

Clyde obliges by hitting him hard with rolling punches. Pablo bends at the knees and tries to fold up but Charlie has him by the arms and is not letting him get away. Clyde lowers his assault by punching on Pablo's cock. Pablo's uncut rod is rock hard. With each slap the cock bounces back to attention and Pablo winces. Clyde reaches down and grabs Pablo's ball sac and pulling it tight really starts Pablo squirming by beating it on it rhythmically. Charlie increases his hold on Pablo as Pablo becomes increasing harder to hold on to.

Clyde holds on to Pablo's balls as from his back pocket he pulls a knife. He flicks the switch blade open in front of Pablo's eyes. His eyes open wide. Clyde lowers the knife until it parallel with Pablo's balls.

"How attached to these are you, spic." Clyde takes the point and lightly traces it over Pablo's pulled tight sac. He tries to squirm.

"I wouldn't move if I were you, spic boy, or you will lose them a whole lot sooner than I want you too."

Clyde pulls the balls out and title and lowers the knife to the skin where they attach. Charlie laughs and yells "Do it. Cut his balls over."

Clyde smiles. "Should I?"

Charlie nods. "Yeah. Let's send this Latin piece of shit back over the border in pieces."

The door behind them explodes open with cries of "INS! INS! Everybody on the floor." Three agents in black suits rush into the room flashing badges and guns. Charlie lets Pablo go back like the other two, Pablo's escape is cut short and he is smashed face first into a cement wall as the INS agents demand to know what is going on here.

Charlie and Clyde protest that they were just having some good clean American fun.

One of the agents leans into Clyde and screams, "And you call threatening to cut some guys balls off good clean fun."

Clyde answers, "Yeah. When he don't belong here in the first damn place."

All three are handcuffed and lead from the room. Clyde and Charlie are shoved into one car and Pablo in the back of another.

Pablo tries to ask where he is being taken. "They got it wrong. I am an American citizen. Where am I going?"

His protestations fall on deaf ears.

The INS drive and drive and a couple hours later of going nowhere. They pull up into a driveway. Pulling him from the car and uncuffing him, Pablo asks what is going on.

"Glad we found you safe. Go up the drive. They'll take it from there."

Pablo stumbles up the stone driveway and smiles. Pushing the bed sheet surrounding the site aside, He enters the main compound. The banner reads, "Welcome to Purgatory."

Master McGuinn is sitting full clothing boots resting on the back of the muscle slave. "Have a good leather fantasy, did we?"

Pablo stumbles forward smiling. "They talk too much shit. But the scene was fun. Are my roommates back?

"Saw them go up a little while ago. You'll find your clothes on your bed if I know the committee."

Pablo walks up the stone stairs to his room.

SWINGERS

"Now in this scene, Cheetah comes along and finds the both of you, Tarzan and Jane, tied to chairs in the abandoned shack. The shack is starting to smolder. Can the chimp save you both before the whole thing goes up in flames? That's your motivation, kids."

Chelsea Nichols struggles with the ropes while the make-up people finish touching up her body make-up. She is wearing nothing but a pair of light tan bra and panties.

"Is this much skin really necessary?" she whines at the Film's Director.

The Director leans back in his chair.

"It's the only way we're going to get any one to watch this turkey." He leans back in his chair and yells, "Clear the set."

The make-up artists leave.

"Roll 'em."

Tied securely to the other chair is Tad Lawrence.

Tad used to be a successful child star on a weekly sitcom, but now since he is not an adorable tyke anymore, his opportunities have been less and less. However, his soft baby fat has been worked into hard lean muscle mass with his supple skin stretched tight over every sinew on his body. Right now, his large pecs are pulled even further out by the tight ropes securing him to the chair. He's wearing nothing but a g-string that barely covers the crack of his hairless ass and his ample bulge, this is outlined clearly in leopard print fur. The Director has had ever inch of Tad's body from the neck down shaved clear and a spray tan applied.

"It'll increase receipts at the box office. Make you more attractive to the teen girls," the director explained as an assistant was applying tanning lotion to Tad's six pack abs.

Tad's agent said it would be good for his career. Tied to a cold chair back to back with an almost naked female while spouting inane dialogue? Tad wasn't so sure.

From behind the camera, an animal trainer releases Cheetah toward the tied-up couple.

Tad looks down. In his best b-movie deep he-man voice, he says, "Cheetah. Glad you come! Free us."

The trainer directs Cheetah to jump up and down. Then he orders him to bite through the ropes. Cheetah bites Chelsea instead.

She screams, "This stupid monkey just gave me rabies!"

The director yells "Cut".

With fury in her eyes, Chelsea screams, "Let me out of these ropes, now or I am going to sue! And get this stupid monkey away from me!"

Chelsea doesn't wait around for Tad to be untied. She rushes over to her trailer, the director, producer, and on set doctor following her as she screams and screams.

A crewmember is about to untie Tad when a hand reaches his shoulder.

"Not yet. Don't untie him yet. I'll take care of it."

The crewmember puts the rope down and walks away.

"You look so hot that way. The furry g-string fits you so well," says Tad's boyfriend, Stefan. Stefan's 'Tarzan, Stud of the Jungle' T-shirt stretched tight across his chest.

"You should know. You designed my costume this way."

"Call what you're wearing a costume?"

"Untie me."

Stefan doesn't move.

"Come on. Untie me. I have to get ready for the next scene."

Stefan leans in.

"How do you ask?"

"Oh come on."

"How do you ask?"

"Please."

"Please what?"

Tad looks around. "Not here."

"Please what?"

Whispering Tad says, "Please, Sir."

Stefan smiles and bends down to until Tad. Whispering in his ear, he says, "We're continuing this at home." Tad smiles and stifles himself from laughing.

The Director comes out of Chelsea's trailer. His shirt is damp and he looks like he's aged a lot in the last few minutes. He rushes up as Tad rises from the chair.

"Stefan, what are you doing here? Oh. Yeah. Right. Please make sure he gets dressed. We're wrapping for the day." He steps back and turns around in a circle yelling, "It's a wrap. Go on home."

Tad walks up to him. "Are you okay?"

The director waves him off. "Go home. See you tomorrow."

The director lumbers back to Chelsea's trailer.

Tad starts to walk off toward his trailer when Stefan catches up.

"You always did have a pretty ass."

Inside the trailer, Tad allows the g-string to slip to the floor and heads toward the small shower. Stefan picks it up in his wake and smells it. The beating of the water resounds through the trailer. Stefan tosses the g-string aside and tears off his T-shirt over his head revealing his own six-pack and very hairy chest. He kicks his shoes off toward the couch exposing his bare feet and starts walking toward the shower stepping out his pants and white underwear as he goes. He knocks on the shower door.

"Open up, Tad."

Tad wipes the shampoo from his eyes. "There's not enough room in here to change your mind."

"There's enough room for what I want to do."

Stefan grabs some lube and a condom out of the toilette kit on a small shelf next to the stall.

He opens the door. "Turn around."

Stefan turns Tad around and squeezes him against the wall while occupying the small remaining space. The water streams down on both of their bodies. Dabbing a little lube on his fingers, he finds the entrance to Tad's ass.

"Relax, boy. Give yourself to me."

"Not here. Please Sir. Not here."

"Why not?"

"What if someone walks in? My reputation. My career. We have to be careful."

"I locked the trailer door."

"But it can be opened so easily."

"Besides we've wrapped for the day."

"But Sir..."

"Shut up, boy, and give me that ass. Been staring at all day. All I could do to not take you on set."

Stefan rips the condom open with his teeth and unrolls it over his engorging cock.

"You may be Tarzan out there, but right you're my Jane. Open up jungleboy and we'll go native."

Tad pushes his round ass forward and Stefan slips in. Stefan holds Tad hands firmly against the wall as he slips in and out of Tad's firm butt. Low moans of ecstasy mix with the beats of the water against skin and shower.

In a low groan, Tad grunts, "Thank You Sir. Please..."

"Please what, jungleboy. You want me to drag your wet ass out here and fuck you harder, pig? Do you?"

"Yes Sir."

Stefan kicks the shower door open and wiggles out from behind Tad. With his right hand he pushes the bottles off the vanity. They fall to the floor in a clatter. With his left he drags Tad by the hair and shoves him over the vanity ass up in the air shoving his face into the mirror. Like a jungle ape, he reimpales Tad's ass fucking him even more vigorously as before.

"Hard enough for you, boy?"

Tad moans loudly. "Yes Sir. Thank You Sir. Please. Please."

"Please, what pig?"

"Fuck the cum out of me."

"Not yet, pig. Not yet."

Stefan continues to work Tad's ass. Until he kicks the shower door closed with his foot and leans back with a rattle in the door. Ordering

Tad down, Tad spins around and kneels as Stefan unloads stream after stream of white cum all over Tad's pecs. The jungleboy receives it rubbing salvo after salvo into his skin and begging for more.

Stefan whips off the last few drops onto Tad and whips a towel at him. "Dry me off pig and then I might let you cum."

Tad does as he is told and after wiping himself down briefly, he and Stefan head into the living room. The door is rattling as someone knocks furiously.

"Dammit, Tad, they told me you haven't left yet. Open the door. I need to talk to someone," screams Chelsea as she tries to tear the door open.

Stefan walks up and hands Tad his robe with the film's logo emblazed on the back. "Told you I locked it and the lock would hold."

Tad slips it quickly on. He walks up to the door grabbing a pair of shorts on a hook nearby and slipping them on under the robe.

"One minute, Chelsea."

Stefan waves and heads into the bedroom closing the door behind himself. Tad glances over and sees the mess in the bathroom. He closes the bathroom door and rushes over to open the trailer door.

"And where have you been? I've been banging for twenty minutes."

"Sorry I was in the shower and didn't hear you. What's up, Chelsea?"

"Did I interrupt something?"

Tad tries not to glance at the bedroom door. "Oh...no...not at all."

Chelsea looks at the door and back at Tad who is sitting crossed legged on the couch trying to hide his crotch under the folds of the bathrobe.

She smiles.

"This can wait. See you tomorrow."

Chelsea walks up to the bedroom door and knocks. She says through it, "See you tomorrow, Stefan." She winks and blows Tad a kiss.

Tad laughs.

"Silly boy. Did you really think we all don't know? Don't worry. None of us are going to tell." On that, she exits the trailer letting it go bang behind her.

Tad walks over to the door and locks it laughing once more.

He walks over to the bedroom and opens the door.

Stefan is still naked. He has rope restraints set up on all four ends of the bed.

"Always did think Chelsea was smarter than they gave her credit for. Come here jungleboy I'll show you what erupts when I tie a man up."

IN SERVICE TO MASTER

The Harley speeds in the darkness in between the flickers of the sparsely spaced street lamps. This slave rides blindfolded with my hands cuffed around a motorcycle. His thick steel cockring hanging off the left epaulet, gleaming and jangling as we go. The smell of the cold wind rushes past my face, but not before passing through the unmistakable mix of Sir's leather and strong musk creating exhilaration unimaginable.

About a week ago, the slave surrendered itself and all its possessions to the pleasures and ownership of Master. I was christened 7, its Master's given name because its born name is now irrelevant. The key in the collar's lock was broken before witnesses in the huge dungeon room of the notorious Gold Coast. Before this slave quit its job, it was a freelance reporter for magazines and some newspapers with a nose for the strange, unique crime. Not the common mob hit or the drunken brawl leading to murder of brother on brother, but I wrote about to what made really great headlines, the truly bizarre. This translated into several books on my exploits and memberships in some of the prestigious mystery/ literary circles. Now Master has ordered that I use my writing skills to write about him and how in his glory and infinite power and wisdom, the slave is allow little problems to solve from time to time. He has also granted this slave use of the first person but only in the written word. "It takes less time to tell the story, slave," he says. "Leave the groveling and self debasement for times at my feet, slave."

Sir is very generous. This weekend we are going to our first post-collaring private night out at his favorite dungeon. He always promises I will build him his own dungeon someday.

My ass aches from the butt plug he placed there slamming back every time we go over a bump in the road. Like to imagine that it is Master's mighty cock instead. Exhaust. Fresh cut grass. The smell of Master's sweat mixed the leather jacket on his strong back. The cool wind hitting us as the bike makes sharp twists and turns as it speeds on through the night. I could go with Master like this forever.

A couple more turns and we stop underneath a bright street lamp. Master unlocks one side of the cuffs and gets off the bike. "Don't let the butt plug come out," he orders. I couldn't if I wanted to. It is jammed in the hole tight. He uncuffs my other hand and slowly lifts me from the bike, holding on to me tightly. I stand, weaving to and fro as the equilibrium comes back. I clutch onto his closed motorcycle jacket. Inside my head spins as if coming down from a tremendous orgasm. He kisses me on the forehead.

"Are you okay, slave?"

"Yes Sir."

He leaves me leaning against the bike. The compartment on the back of the bike clicks, and he gives me the toy bag from inside and then attaches to my collar his Harley dog leash. Master then locks up the bike and tugs on the leash for me to follow.

Master removes the blind fold and tells me to open my eyes slowly. My eyes take time to adjust to the light, what light there was. Behind us, the entranceway was still open and the moonlight drifted into the opening, but before us was impenetrable darkness. Master drops the leash, orders me to kneel, and walks into the darkness.

The door closes, eliminating the last of the light. A single light comes on above, revealing a table hanging from a frame by chains. Master reappears and pats me on the head. "Bring the bag over to the table, slave." Master walks back into the dark and the illumination on the light gets brighter. On the edge of the light is a small wooden cube. Master orders me to lay the bag on the cube and strip.

The ropes rub against my skin as he ties me to the table. My slave cock begins to rise. Master grabs my cock gives it a couple jerks and then gently slaps me across the face.

"Getting excited, slave? Don't remember giving permission for that." Master's gloved hands rub over his property.

The next two hours are delicious pain. Slowly, Master loads his slave's cock and balls with light clothespins until it is covered as it could be. The pain shoots from my genitals through my body in jolts. Some of the rubbing of the clothespins is beginning to make the underside of my scrotum burn. Then, Master starts to line my tender inner thighs. I feel his gentle touch as he places each clothespin. He is no hurry and has no reason to be for He rented the dungeon for all night. He pats my head. "More's coming, slave."

With a crackle, the ultra violet wand zaps my nips and the head of my engorged clothespin covered cock. The shock runs in through my nipple rings and down my arms. The smell of burning comes from the slave's nether regions. Master pats me on the head and tells me it is going to be all right. The ropes chafe against my body, but I am tied down and there is no leeway.

He pulls the rough backside of his hand down between my pecs and through my belly back down to the crotch. "Ready?" He strikes at the clothespins on my cock sending them flying as I let out a piecing scream. Tears well up in my eyes. "Ready to go again? Slave?"

Somehow I mutter, "Yes Sir." It feels like the skin is being ripped away.

"Do you want me to continue or be nice and take them off one at a time?"

"Please, Sir." Tears stream down my face. I would like to curl up but the ropes keep me down firmly.

He continues to take them off, now pulling them violently in twos and threes as he allows his slave to whimper openly. He stops and kisses my forehead. Leaning next to my ear, Master whispers, "I love watching you suffer and knowing that you can't make it stop...ever." Master reaches down and grabs what I hope is the last of the clothespins, a whole bunch on the edge of the shaft and yanks. Reflex has me trying to jerk up from the table but I go nowhere. The pins are pushed away and the bonds begin to loosen, sliding off me.

"Don't move, slave." Master lifts me down from the table. I pull myself to my knees and kiss and lick his boots loving in gratefulness. Something lands with a loud thud next to my head. "Good slaves get rewards. Look next to you." It is a new mystery novel by Sue Grafton.

"Some day, slave, we will find some other use for your inquisitive mind."

SURVIVING MASTER'S HELL

Daddy spins the young yuppie, ripping his shirt off as he turns and then body slams him into the wall. He was soon naked, wearing only his socks and boots. The yuppie's jeans, underwear and shirt were lying in ripped shreds on the cell floor. Daddy pushes the yuppie down to his knees. "Slave, teach him how to behave. Lick my slave's boots then suck his dick." The yuppie nods his head no. Daddy grimaces as his biceps tighten. He kicks the yuppie's knees out from under him and he ends up flat faced on the floor. "Do what my slave tells you!"

"Daddy says for you lick to my boots. You better take that tongue of yours and lick them clean," I tell the convicted yuppie now naked at my feet. Daddy stands with his massive tattooed arms folded. The yuppie pokes his tongue slowly out of his mouth and lightly touches it to the toe of my boot. I take the back of my other boot and jam his head into the leather.

Daddy laughs, giving me a pat on the head and glaring down as he says, "Get licking, pussy boy." He glares up at me and through angry teeth the yuppie warns me that he could make my life hell. I give him a big toothy smile back down at him. "In here, it is different. Do what you're told and Daddy will protect you." The yuppie gives my boots a lick and then another. He has no idea, I thought, of what hell really is. It wasn't until much later that I could tell him, but right now he was learning how to serve.

I sat him down later when Daddy was done with both of us.

After Daddy had his fill of us having sex with each other, having sex with us, and fucking our asses after filing our asses with squirt after squirt of his seed, while still inside of us. I told him about how lucky he really is. I didn't have to learn for Daddy. I have had the honor and pleasure of serving one Sir and another for many years. It was an honor to lick their boots, pits and ass, to serve as their ashtray or foot stool or to know that I was serving them their favorite drink or meal. He looks at me drained with puppy eyes. I pick up the yuppie's head and kiss him lightly on the lips. Giving him a small hug I reassure him that all will be okay. "If Daddy accepts you, we will be brothers," I whisper in his ear. He whines, how could things be worse? "They can always be worse. Why do you think I'm here?" Even in the safety of Daddy's arms, even there, I go back time and time again. Back to a time in my life when it was worse.

Under the brightness of the beams of the moonlight, I run through the shadowy cornfield barefoot and naked. The corn stalks rub against my sensitive skin and the downed stalks and small rocks crunch and bite into the bottom of my feet. I'm better off leaving it all behind and the faster the better. All I could think of was escape and so far I am free. But he'll be after me, so I got to keep running and hiding. Maybe I ought to head for town. Someone there is sure to help me. Maybe I can get picked up by the police for being naked in public. That is at least something. Something, anything that isn't him. I am hungry and tired but the deep scarring whip marks across my chest, back, buttocks, and thighs remind me with every movement of my muscles that I've got to keep running. I can see him bending over my cage after leaving me there for a week to sit in my own filth and bending over to find my permanent collar sawed through and the file underneath my disgusting tattered bedding. I took nothing because as his slave I had nothing. The stars twinkle and the lightning bugs light and spin through the air from among the stalks, but I have no time to waste. I'm running from the whipping sessions that seemed to go on for hours, the desperate cries for him to stop until my tear ducts no longer watered, and the blood, my own, running over my body and the cold, cold water coming from his metal bucket to wash it off. I'm running because of the hernia I was hospitalized for because he wouldn't stop putting weights in the boot hanging from my balls despite my screams. Running from being pissed and crapped on and told the toilet was better than I was.

This wasn't how I had come to love this life. My life was leather and latex, bondage and discipline, sleeping at foot of his bed, appropriate punishments, and ultimately being told that I was a "good slave." The nights in the loving care of a dominant who not only beat and used me, but cared for his property seemed long gone, a very distant memory. I'd now sell my soul for one caress, one tender touch, one positive word.

Oh, I have tried to get away before. Once he caught up with me

on the main road. That's why I am sticking to the cornfields along side roads. He beat me mercilessly and I wasn't allowed to eat or evacuate myself for a week. The hardest thing is not to throw up as your own feces backs up into your stomach and system. He looked down at me in my locked cage and said if I did I would eat every drop, and I knew he would be as true as his word.

Before him, I remember kneeling at a Sir's boots being lightly slapped with his leather gloved hand, getting lost in the smell as his musk mixing with the sweat and the leather and the smell of the stogie hanging from his lips. Starting at the toe of his boot, I would make small circles with my tongue, going until the boot was covered and I would try to work my way up his chaps, seeing how high Sir would let me explore with my tongue. But now I need to run and hide. I don't go after any cars. I might make a mistake. It might be his car, if he has one. My place is the dungeon. I wasn't good enough to be allowed upstairs or anywhere else in his life. I was his toy to use and abuse. No pleasure for me, for it was the torment and pain in my eyes that pleased him most. If Sir had a bad day at work, I got the beating. If Sir was horny, there I am. I was his for every punch, whip, strike, vulgar word, to take his pain and be used only for his pleasure, no matter how well I was. I had no business being tired or sick in his mind. What I felt, thought or needed – all were irrelevant. I was his piece of shit slave and I better obey or suffer the consequences. And suffer them I did. Not a day went by without a beating, flogging or whipping to the level of bloodiness and many times beyond that.

Who knows what the hell he'll do if he catches me this time? Keep on running. I can see my breath as it comes from my contracting pecs and hits the cold night air. Spit freezes to my unshaven face. The cold pierces my tendered overly-stretched nips that have been tortured excessively and stand far away from my body.

Lights. In the distance, I see the lights of town. At least, I think it is town. Maybe I can find the police station and turn him in. I've got to keep going. Stumbling. Running. But going. Got to keep going. Do I dare stop and catch my breath? Weak. Can't even think about the weakness or the hunger. All this corn all around me. I can eat corn at least. No. Got to keep going. Will eat later. I've waited a week. I can wait longer.

A crossroads. I look each way and run quickly across the pavement. Looking around, I hope no one saw me. I hope he didn't see me. I lay down in the drainage gully beside the road. My heart beats heavily in my chest. I need to rest for a second and only a second. It seems like I've been running for days but it has only been hours. Lights down the road. A car. I dash quickly the few feet and take a flying leap far into the corn stalks. They pierce my body like his unwelcome needle play piercing my body. I stifle my scream. Quiet is what is needed. Be quiet or it's my life. What a choice.

When I first talked to him online he seemed so different. At last, I thought I had found a real Master in the vast sea of Internet wannabes. We e-mailed, called, and IM'd back and forth for at least three months. Then I lost my job. My home was surely next. Maybe I rushed it. He seemed so wonderful. He invited me for a visit and an interview. A visit I never went home from. He seemed so genuine on-line and over the phone. I thought I was safe. No reason to tell anyone where I was going. I judged him safe. Besides, I'd be back on Monday. That Monday was a long time ago.

The lights get closer. It is a dark colored Buick. It doesn't slow down. It roars past. I stop holding my breath. I stay on this side and head toward the far away lights. Can I crunch quieter? Seas of corn stalks. Those lights don't seem to be getting nearer, but I must be making progress. Maybe another hour or maybe two. I don't know, but I've got to keep going,

Lights again down the road. They come closer. A cop car. It's a fucking cop car. I let out a sigh of relief. Maybe he will help. Maybe he'll arrest me for public nudity. At least I'll end up with a blanket, food, and even medical care. Jumping up, I run into the middle of the road.

It's nighttime but I know that my naked light skin will reflect in his headlights. Come on, arrest me. At least, I'll be safe from him. The car gets me in its headlights and stops a few feet from me. My spirit is free. I'm already for your handcuffs. All I am thinking is cuff me...throw me in back...I'm naked...save me...arrest me. I'll resist arrest. Anything you want, take me with you. For the first time in a long time my spirit soars. Thank you, God! I feel only joy and exultation.

The cop's thigh high boots land with a crunch on the road as he exits the car. They shine brightly in the light of the headlights. He walks up to me in shadow but as the moonlight begins to shine on his face, my heart sinks. I turn to run but he takes his long black baton off him belt and smashes me full force in the stomach. As I bend over, he smashes me in the back and I'm flat on the pavement. He kicks me with the full force of the front of his boot and begins to stomp on my back and arms and legs trading off with kicking, spitting on me, and whacking me with his baton cursing all the time.

Damn! He's a cop. Master's a fucking cop. He handcuffs my hands behind my back in the lightning speed that cops can and he kicks me to the side of the road where the beating continues until blood comes pouring out of the cuts on my body and from my mouth. He takes out his dick out and pisses on me from head to toe. He then flogs me with corn stalks he pulls out of the ground with the rush of adrenaline that courses through his body. Swearing at me and telling me how worthless I am, he throws me in the trunk of the cop car and slams down the lid. The slam reverbs in my ears and my total body bleeds and aches. I try to cry only to hear something come crashing against the back seat and an order to "shut the fuck up, you worthless piece of shit." The road bumps along underneath and ever inch of hope drains from my bloody body.

He takes me back to my own personal hell. Needless to say, I lost more weight through more starvation. I was cuffed against a wall like a prisoner in the Middle Ages in an old Hollywood movie. There I stayed. I think it might have been two weeks. It felt like an eternity, but all his punishments feel that way. My legs ached. My back ached for me to sit down and I couldn't. Soon, my bladder couldn't empty anymore because there was nothing left to empty in it.

Eventually, he let me down and threw me in a new cage. He was pissed that he had to buy a new one. I don't even remember the beating that followed. I was left on bread and water and then suddenly a new diet item, dog food. Even the dog food was too good for me, he said. Days went by. He'd fuck me and complain that I was getting too thin and soon he would have to throw me in a hole in the back yard and let me die from my worthless life if I didn't gain weight and please him. Things did get a little better. He soon fed me the dog food twice daily and I was allowed a lot of water. He still said he could not trust me and that he would make sure I never disobeyed him again.

I did try to escape a few more times, but I was no secret. Each time he or his buddies on the force returned me as "his property." "I think this belongs to you," they would say as they handed me back over with a sneer.

Something held within me. Sometimes I don't know how. I felt worthless. I remembered all the good times when S&M would send me in endorphin highs and the pats on the head. "You're a good slave," a Sir would say with a gloved hand.

I always thought being in service to a cop would be a great leather fantasy. Sort of a kinky slave to an Andy Taylor or a Sipowicz with a kinky streak. "Please, Sir, let me grease your nightstick," I would squeal and beg. This was not a cop even like on Cops. He was a monster with a badge. His uniform stretched over his large taut muscles but the dominance and hate poured from his eyes and he took his frustrations with the criminal and court systems out on me with his whip, belt, the back of his hand and sometimes even his fists while a stream of that day's frustrations poured from his mouth like water from a faucet.

I lost teeth. He broke bones and I had bruises inside and out. He would tell the hospital people that I was a vagrant he found on the street. I had no insurance, so they treated me and released me back to him in his care. What a joke. "Released in his care."

He believed in spit but not in lube. My asshole was raw as a side of beef. If I complained, he'd thrust harder and deeper, filling my hole with every shot of his cum and when he felt like it, loads of his piss. When days were especially bad, he would say that if he had to eat shit then, I did. He'd squat on a dish and that would be my "banquet," and he'd take pleasure in my eating every piece.

What kept me alive? Hell if I know. Maybe the hope that someday this would end or I would be dead. As sure I am telling this story, it did end. It had to end. I want to return to this life as I had known it. The glory of being used and serving a man whom actually gave a shit, but first I had to be free of him.

One night, he forgot to lock the cage. I turned over in my fetal position and it swung open with the touch of what was left of the raw blistered sole of my right foot. I stretched out my legs and heard the bones pop back into alignment. I crawled out of the cage. No noise. Make no noise. Circling the dungeon slowly, I tried to decide what to do. Try to escape again? No, I would only be caught again and this hell would only continue. I crept slowly up the wooden stair that I always saw him come down. The stairwell I dreaded because I knew it was only about to continue every time I saw him come down it. The door wasn't locked. It had been rare times that I was up here in his space, usually only when I was trying to escape. A space he had said many times had a no slaves allowed rule, but I was out. Running would do no good. I had to finish this. I roamed the hallways like a wild animal escaped from his cage in the zoo.

Upstairs, I found his bedroom. I opened the door so the noise would not disturb him. He was sound asleep. His head rested on a few pillows and he was tucked inside a brightly colored comforter. His cop clothes were hanging over a chair and his boots sat tall underneath the chair. I glanced quickly around the room. His truncheon was sitting on the bureau. I slipped it out of his leather belt hanger. My fingers curled around its wooden base. I crept over to his bed. He looked so peaceful. He snored gently and looked like he would never harm a fly. I raised the truncheon over my head. Breathing in, I brought it down with every ounce of strength I had left in my body. With the first blow to the head, he awoke and started screaming but the adrenaline was coursing through my veins and all I could think was of him dead. He tried to get up but I kept swinging and swinging and soon he started bleeding just like I had from all of his beatings and tortures. But the steady string of threats and vulgarisms kept coming from his mouth, so I bashed. Soon, both of us and the bed were covered in his blood. He needs to die or I am going to die. I bashed him until he couldn't speak and couldn't move. His strong face lost its good looks. I bashed his legs and his arms. He wasn't going to move and come after me again. He tried to lift himself to come after me, but I kept up the attack. I kept it up until he was good and dead. I threw the truncheon down next to the bed. I was free of the son of a bitch once and for all. I celebrated. I went down into the kitchen and ate his food. I didn't even stop to wash off the blood. Each bite felt like a banquet. I even left dirty dishes in the sink. Take that.

The state police found me in answer to my call. Believe me, I wasn't going to call his buddies on the local cops. I told them everything. I sat there on the bed, his bed, covered in his blood. He lay on his side with his eyes and mouth open, silent and motionless. I didn't feel like crying. They busted into the house and found me sitting there. See what I did? Me? The worthless piece of shit slave? Some of his cop buddies were indicted in complicity. I cooperated. I answered all their questions like a good slave. The state cops got me new clothes. I even got regular meals and medical attention. I overheard the doc tell them that I was within weeks of starving to death.

I still have regular meals and clean clothes. Okay, so they're all orange jumpers and boots. I even get to wear underwear and socks. The day they gave them to me, I cried. The cops at the gate wanted me to turn over my possessions. I laughed. I had nothing and wanted nothing from my former Master's place.

I have a new Daddy. Met him here in prison. He makes sure I eat and that I'm safe. He even helped me get a TV and books for my cell. I forgot what I was like to read and relax watching television. All I know is there is no more bad torment. I still expect this dream to end, but when I wake in morning and the cell doors open, he's there for me. He even fucks me with what lube he can get and he's actually gentle. Even imprisoned for murder, here in jail, I am safe, healthy, cared for and most importantly, free.

I hold the yuppie now shaking before me and hold him tight. "That isn't going to happen to you. You're here with Daddy and I and our life together. Even in this place there is love and freedom." I wipe the tears from his eyes. "Even in here one can cherish what it is like to be safe and in a strange way to be free."

Daddy wakes up from his bunk and with a stretch of mighty arms and well-defined chest, he roars, "Well slaves, hope you got your rest. Come here and suck my dick."

BLACK CROSS – NEW MEXICO

The last dying rays of the sun glow over the desert's surface. The grains of sand between the sparse vegetation take on a sparkle like the stars, twinkling in the emerging night sky. The sun slowly sets, leaving streaks of red, yellow, and brown on the horizon. Standing alone in the middle of this desert, away from the cacti and the ground plants, is a large, thick, black wooden cross. Many similar crosses can be found across the landscape in this part of the country, however, this symbol is unique. Not only because of the relative thickness of the wood used, or the isolation in this part of the desert, or its deep blackness against the fading light of the surroundings, but because a naked man is tied to it by strands of strong hemp rope. His taut body begins to steam from the heat of his sun reddened skin. The naked man leans, draped over the cross like a rag doll. The strength of the cross seems to be the only way he is keeping himself standing upright. He has long since stopped struggling again the bonds that hold him fast. The deep marks of the ropes can be seen on his wrists and ankles. His back, butt and the back of his legs are a mix of red, blue and purple, covered in blisters partially from the heat of the sun and the healed short streaks left by a long time at the end of a single tail. His face is unshaven, haggard, gray and weary, with a look in his eyes that only registers not anger or pain but resolution to his fate.

In the distance, there's a small rumbling. The object blends with the ever-darkening surroundings. His sizzled skin burns as he tries to crane his neck for one small glimpse of the strange sound in the all too wide expanse.

Two white specks appear along the horizon. The rumbling becomes a type of crunching like stone being crushed underneath the feet of some great black creature slowly making its way across the great desert.

The naked man shifts on his feet. He has been standing for many hours. He curls his toes and bends his legs to work through the constant cramping from inside his muscles and gut. He didn't piss because it's been hours since the man gave him his last sips of water and he is trying to force his body to reuse its usually discarded moisture. His stomach growls. The noise gets louder as the white speaks become recognizable beams. They are the lighted eyes of a great black truck. The man gazes up to the heavens. The sun has almost totally disappeared over the horizon. The sky has taken on a dark blue hue and the stars have started to increase in appearance. The moon slowly makes its way up in the sky from behind the clouds that block its light from illuminating the floor of the desert below.

The large black truck careens its last few yards toward the cross. Like an animal examining its prey, it quickly circles the man and the cross, kicking up dust and dirt as it goes spinning around and around revolution after revolution. The truck pulls up behind the naked figure and stops. The vehicle sits silent; its headlights stare straight, illuminating some of the ground clutter ahead. A desert rabbit looks up and scurries away. The engine sputters and stops. Once again, all is still in the desert except maybe for the blowing of a small breeze and the low chirping of crickets.

The driver's side door opens, creaking loudly in the stillness. A pair of dirty black leather cowboy boots land on the ground with a crunch, kicking up a small cloud of sand and dust. A cigar butt gets thrown to the ground and is stomped out by toe of a well-worn cowboy boot.

The driver is a well-muscled man. He wears both handcuffs and a long black flogger from his left side. his round, firm ass is packed into a pair of tight fitting well-worn jeans that also shows a long bulge going down his right leg. His open plaid flannel shirt reveals hard pecs covered in a graying mass of hair. The brim of Peterbilt hat protects his eyes from the dust and sand. Stoking his bushy mustache, he makes his way around the truck. He stops in front of the cross. Taking a small circular box from his back pocket, he takes some chewing tobacco and places it in his cheek. He stands there, arms folded, and then begins to pace back and forth while staring at the figure who is slowly becoming a silhouette in the night.

Strolling back to his truck, he pulls out a long flashlight from behind the driver's seat and slams the truck door with a noise that reverberates in the open desert. He walks back to the cross and shines the light on the backside of the naked man. The naked man limply picks up his head and tries to look back at him. He is welcomed by a backhand slap across the back of his head and his face shoved into the cross. The naked man lets his head droop to one side. The flashlight beam drags along the naked body as he slowly circles. Stopping to look, the naked man gets hits right in the face with the beam of the flashlight. His blinking into the light is rewarded with a large glob of tobacco juice that gets spit into his face. The spit drips down the reddened face and is absorbed away, leaving a black trail down his cheek. He finishes his circle and stops behind the naked man. Gingerly, he takes his hand and strokes his back. He feels the naked man tense up, but he does not try to move away from the pain caused by the sensitivity of the skin. Turning the flashlight around, he smashes its long handle a couple of times in the round hard butt cheeks of the tied man. Then he repeats the act a couple times more. Pulling him by the back of hair, he spits another load of tobacco juice in his face. He then places the flashlight on the back of the truck so it serves as a bright spotlight, illuminating the cross and its inhabitant.

Stepping back, he unclips the flogger from his belt loop. It hangs from his right hand and he gently touches the naked man's back lightly stroking it with the touch of his manly fingers of his left hand. Lightly he caresses the naked man with the tails of the flogger rubbing them gingerly across his muscular naked body. With a jerk he pulls the tails off of him and with a swing over his head, he lets the tails fly within inches of the naked body. The figure on the cross flinches. Another pass and he lightly touches his back with the tips of the flogger. The man doesn't move. Another swing and the tails hit a little harder into the reddened back. Each swing increases in intensity and the naked man does his best not to move, as he knows he shouldn't. After a long while, the flogger is biting into his back and behind with each swing harder and harder in comes down in force until it is hard it seems that it might take his breath away. Swing after swing. Some come to him above and below. Some come from different directions as the man tosses his flogger from hand to hand to keep the strikes coming from different levels and different directions.

"Okay, pig. Ten last ones." These were the hardest of all as he takes both hands of the flogger and wails into the naked man's back with all the force available to him. "One, two, three..." The naked man does his best not to move but he can't help it.

"That doesn't matter what you do. You are taking them all." Six, seven, eight. The naked man grabs into the cross to keep him standing with ever inch of strength still left to keep himself standing upright. Nine. Ten. The last is the hardest of all. The man wipes the sweat from his brow with the bottom of his shirt, leaving it hanging out of his tight pants. He switches the flashlight off and puts it in his back pocket. He places the flogger behind the passenger seat in the truck.

The man walks over to the cross and releases one of the bonds. The naked man stays hanging against the post, trying his best not to move at all. He pulls the naked man against himself holding him still with his massive arm. The naked man feels his hot stinging back as it rubs against the buttons and flannel of his shirt. Pulling the flashlight out of his back pocket, he flicks it on and uses it to examine the man's chest. His nipples have been rubbed raw and are represented by two large scabs. The chest and the front of the legs show the same whip marks as the front. He releases the other bond and the naked man falls into his arms like a limp doll. They stand there motionless as the increasing wind wraps around them. He runs his fingernail down in between the naked man's pecs and through his abs. The naked man can't help his shivering and trembling. He then can feel the body in his arms tense and waits for the punishment for moving. Instead, he slings the naked man over his shoulder and deposits him lying on his face in the back of the truck. The naked man stretches out on the truck bed, trying to make his joints work and feeling the grooves of the cold metal bed against his body. He just stands there, shining the light down into the truck bed, and watched the naked man's movements with amusement. The naked man turns and shields his face from the light. His hand is pulled away from his face and another load of tobacco juice is spit. He gets into the truck bed and shoves the naked man back down on the metal surface. He stands there with the bottom of his boot against the back of his head, making sure that it is ground into the truck bed. Having done that, he cuffs the naked man's hands behind his back. He spits another gob of tobacco juice onto his back.

Jumping off the back of the truck, the man takes his shirt and cap off and throws them behind his seat in the front cab. The wind blows across the thick hair of his tight, muscular chest. From inside the truck, he takes out a large oilcan and something small and plastic wrapped. Walking back to the truck bed, he unbuttons his fly and takes out his engorged dick. Climbing back up on the truck bed, he sticks the nozzle of the can up the butthole of the naked man and begins to move his butt cheeks around. Lube begins to fill the inside and starts to dribble out over the reddened butt cheeks. Ripping open the wrapped packet, he slips the condom on and, with a leap of a coyote on his prey, he plunges into the naked man with one great push. The naked man tries to stifle the scream as he thrusts in and out of his butthole. The thrusts are slow at first, but as his rose begins to open the thrusts increase in speed and violence. The wheels begin to bounce and the underside of the truck begins to squeak as he pounds the hole faster, deeper and harder, moving his hips and own magnificent butt up and down with each thrust. The truck rocks back and forth with the increased power of each thrust. He grunts louder and louder, with each thrust burying his large cock as far as it will go.

123

It is as if he is trying to dig it in so far that it will come out of the naked man's mouth.

He's the primal man, taking through grunts and force what is his to take. Sweat comes flying off their bodies as the anal assault continues. He slows down only to slam back in and assault the rose. For the naked man this may seem to take an eternity, but it is an eternity of lustful pleasure as his own cock rubs up against the metal bed of the truck. Getting hard and erect while his butt is fed massive cock, his body covered in bruises from being smashed with each push and his ass and back being punched in intervals during the thrusts. The smashing, punching and hard fucking continue on and on. With each turn, the naked man's endorphins rise beyond where they have ever risen before, until he can feel it no longer. In fact, it feels like the body on top of his is the only thing keeping him from rising off the truck.

Pulling himself off the naked man with almost a loud wolf howl, he spews a steady stream of white that pierces the darkness with luminescence and covers the butt and backside of the naked man bruised at his feet. It comes in steady streams of rain, covering the naked man in a head to leg blanket of white stickiness. After he is through cumming, he picks up a clean rag from the truck and wipes himself down, starting with the last remaining drops on the very end of his huge uncut dick. After wiping the sweat off of his pecs, pits, and massive toned chest, he throws the rag down next to the naked man but commands him not to move. He pulls his pants, throwing them down into the truck bed. He pulls the naked man out of the truck bed and forces him face first into the dirt. Pulling another condom out from his truck and casting the wrapper to the wind, he slips it on and resumes the violent fucking, plunging deeper and harder. The naked male body feels each thrust throughout and the sharp crunch of the sand and rocks as they eat into flesh. His hands begin to come down and smack the reddened checks sending pain with each ever increasing thrust. The man is the bronco and he is being given the ride of his life. The pounding lasts longer this time and is even more relentless than before. The dirt blows up around them both as it mixes with their sweat.

He stops, pulls his cock out and throws off the condom into the dark desert night. One stroke and the naked man is once more being covered with load after load of cum. He kicks the naked man over and finishes cumming on his front and then washes it off by the golden stream of piss he uses to drench the man. Leaving him to soak in the night and lie in the dirt and dust, the man goes to get his pants and slips them back on over his boots. Zipping up his fly, he returns to the truck. Sitting in the cab with the door open, he pulls a beer can from the seat next to him, spits the remaining tobacco on the desert floor and tags a big swig of beer. Sighing, he leans back and glares at the figure on the ground. He takes another swig. He pulls the shirt out and wipes the sweat off of his chest, belly and pits. He goes to the back of the truck. Walking back to the figure of the ground, he grinds the man's face into the dust with the heel of his boot, making him eat dirt off the desert floor.

A coyote howls in the distance at the moon. He tosses the empty beer can into the night, now pitch dark except for the moon, stars, and lights of the truck. "You fuckin' whore." He kicks the prone figure. "Take that pig. Shut up and take it like the fuckin' piece of dirt you are." He keeps violently kicking him again and again. The figure remains still, bracing his body for each blow of the steel capped cowboy boot toe. The curses and insults fall toward the ground with the veracity of each kick. It stops as quickly as it started, as if his lack of response is no fun for the dominant man. The naked man's breathing turns back to regular as he relaxes.

"Get your ass up!" the man commands him. The naked man pushes himself as the man kicks him with the bottom of his boot and he collapses back to the ground. "C'mon, pig. You've already wasted much of my day and night. No more. Move it." The naked man struggles to his knees and elbows, and then to his feet. Swaying, the man guides him to the back of truck. The naked man is lifted into the back of the truck body and recuffed with the discarded handcuffs. Jumping out, the man closes the back end and returns to the cab. He slides the small door in the back window. "Had a good birthday, pig? "Had enough? Happy birthday, fuckhead. Things I do for you, you whiny fuckin' slave." The door slides back as the slave's answer is unimportant.

A small noise and the big metal creature comes back to life. With a large jerk, the truck rolls forward and the naked man and his captor drive away into the night, crunching the desert rocks as they go.

THE KIDNAPPING

Mark smirks at me from under his bushy mustache as I walk in the door. Plopping down on the stool, he pushes the $1 beer he's already poured toward me. I take a swig and chat him up. So far today it's been slow for him but the night is only starting. I finish the beer and he pours me another. Two hot muscle guys are taking turns at the pinball machine in the next room. Both sport military buzzcuts and jeans stretched so tight it looks like it could cut off the circulation to their big hard butts. The noise from the banging of the ball against the bumpers, the dinging of the scoreboard and their excited shouting is the only noise in this too quiet leatherbar. Excusing myself, I head to the bathroom.

When I head back from the toilet, I look over and the two guys aren't at the machine. It's okay. That type is never interested in me. I swallow a couple big gulps of beer. Mark answers the phone turning his back to me. I pull the Marlboro packet out from my upper jacket pocket and light up a smoke. What happened next, I remember sort of. I remember putting the cigarette down and tossing my Marlboro box on to the bar and taking one more sip of beer. A cup of sips more and everything started to get hazy. It usually takes a lot more than this to get me drunk. Then, pain and lots of it. I am shoved full force into the bar as my right arm is twisted behind me. Everything starts to go black. I believe a blindfold was slipped over my eyes, but all I can focus on is the pain shooting through out my body. Suddenly, it stopped because the darkness overtook me and my consciousness was gone.

I wake up to the smell of leather. I try to open my eyes and move my head but I can't do either. My head has been encased in a hood and somehow it has been fastened to the floor. I am lying on a blanket and feel the smoothness of the one over me as well. My body still aches from the assault. I try to lift my hand to rub myself but a restraint keeps it fastened down. I am spread eagle restrained to the bottom of the van as well. My mind races. What happened? What the hell am I doing here? Think. Think. Air rushes around whatever I am in. Crunching noise from below me. I must be in a car or truck, maybe an SUV. How long have I been out? I could be in another state, another country. I could be anywhere. Oh my God! No one's going to look for me until I don't show up at the store until tomorrow. My parents are at convention in Las Vegas. My brother's training with the reserves. No one will miss me until it might be too late. I try to scream but the gag is in and all I can do is make unintelligible mumble. Struggling against the bonds also turns out to be a wasted effort. I try to push up but there is a strap holding my waist down as well. My bare leg is touching what feels like a plastic bag. My dick and ass feel full. Those bastards plugged and catharized me! I try to scream and struggle. It is just no good.

Wait. There was that guy. In the chatroom, there was that guy. He was a blonde hairy muscled body builder. He told me he has a big black lover who was also a bodybuilder. They were personal trainers. That's right. They were personal trainers. He asked me if I ever wanted to be kidnapped and forced to be trained. This can't be happening. I joked back something like "Sure. Sounds fun." I exercise but I'm no body builder. I have a thin tight body with small pecs and respectable sprinkling of chest hair. But they wouldn't go to this extent. Besides you can never go by anything anyone says in a chat room. That can't be it. Still here I am. Somebody put something in my drink, probably when I was in the can. Still who would want me out of the way this badly?

I lied there for a long time. Could have been minutes but it felt like hours. My body felt numb. Couldn't feel my arms, legs or anything after a while. I guess I passed out again because when I came I was on a soft cot wrapped in a blanket in what seemed like a totally dark room. Mysterious hands were rubbing me all over and low voices were mumbling about getting my circulation going and that I had been tied down too long. I closed my eyes again. I didn't want whoever it was to know that I was awake and conscious.

A deep voice, I think he sounded like he was African American said, "This boy is a better start than the last pig."

A nasal voice agreed saying that in time I could be another valuable part of the stable. What kind of stable? I wanted to open my eyes and protest but I was scared of what would happen next. A few feet away, I heard the jangle of keys and loud creaking of a door opening. The keys struck the door and I could here the loud clang of what I supposed was bars. The two guys picked up the cot and moved it into the waiting cage. A loud clang and a sharp click as the lock is thrown.

The African American spoke again. "Slave, watch him. Scream loud when he awakens. The very second he does."

A meek voices answers, "Yes Sir." He puts a rough wool blanket over me.

He bends over me. "Wake up my newest little brother. Wake-up and greet the Masters. You'll like it here. They take good care of all of us." The slave brushes my hair from off my face. His touch is gentle. The drug whatever it was has not all together worn off. I turn over grateful for the ability to finally move. I roll into the blanket and sleep takes me away once more. He laughs softly.

"Then sleep, little brother. Tomorrow you'll see. The Masters only make us better."

He takes a corner of the blanket and lies next to me cradling me in his arms.

The next morning or what I assume might be, I sit up in the cot. The cage door is wide open. The cage itself is as high as the room and fills and entire corner of it. I am quite alone and my eyes adjust quickly to the dark. Next to me is a small carton of milk and a bologna sandwich. I am in a dungeon and the cage is at one side of a massive room. My stomach growls. I eat the meal while looking around. It isn't a bad looking place. Everything from ceiling beams to the equipment is made of mahogany and walnut. Whoever these guys are they have money. I have been stripped of all my clothes except for a black jockstrap. I am dying for a smoke but there aren't even any ashtrays around.

I find the stairs out of the dungeon and surprisingly the door at the top of them is wipe open. I turn the corner into a stainless steel kitchen. The only items on the counter in large containers of protein powders and supplements an expensive blender. I turn around to see a large "no smoking" sign. Is this the sight of the real torture? In the room walks a thin but powerfully built muscle guy. He couldn't be more than 25 or 26 and built like a mini brick shithouse.

"You're awake. Wait right here. Wait!"

He runs off.

I walk out of the kitchen door and into the yard.

Barnyard and cornfields for as far as the eye can see. Nothing in the yard except for chickens and one cow looking at me with boredom in its eyes. A voice booms out behind me, "So slave where is he?"

I take off running toward a barn in the distance. Maybe I can hide there during the day and at night I can make my way to a town and get home.

On entering, it turned out to be like any barn I had ever seen. There was a hayloft and a ladder leading to it, but that's where the similarities ended. It stark sterile white inside. The chrome of the workout equipment gleaming and computers lined one wall waiting to make various computations. The cow didn't live here in the winter or at any time. Metal clanged and from a distant corner, I saw him rise from the weight bench. He was even more magnificent looking. He was wearing a tight pair of white gym shorts, socks, and trainers. His body was covered with light blonde hair and dripping in sweat. He came toward me with a gait that projected power.

"Finally up. You had orientation yet, slave?"

I couldn't speak. I couldn't move. The door behind me blasted open.

"Rufus, stop that. It gets expensive replacing those doors."

"Sorry, Gerhard, but this one ran."

"Did you run, slave?"

I didn't know where to look. I was trapped between two muscle gods both stripped to the waist and angry with me. The one called Gerhard spoke at me again.

"Why did you run, slave. Thought you wanted to be trained?"

I mumbled, "I do."

With those words Rufus advanced. I tried to back a way but with one swing of his massive arm, he scooped me up and threw me over his shoulder and carried me from the barn.

The next few hours were different from any slave application I've ever made. He measured my body fat through measuring equipment and a breathing apparatus. Took blood and urine samples. Rufus pushed me to do pushups until I could do anymore then he did the same with sit-ups until my stomach cramped so much all I could was rollover in pain.

"One more exam, slave." He threw a pair of sneakers and a pair of white shorts at me and ordered me to put them on. My body was hooked to heart monitor and then he put a belt on me. In the middle of the cornfield, a road had been carved out. The sun was started to going down and my chest pulled back against the encroaching cold. He didn't care. He hooked the belt to the back of a Honda. Rufus slapped me on the ass and snarled in my eye, "You'll keep running if you know what's good for you." The car started up and off we went with me struggling to keep up the pace. No catching up my breath. Running, running and more running. At first, he went slowly. I got into a rhythm. It wasn't too bad, but with every other lap or so, he kicked up the speed a little. The corn stalks crunched under my feet and the tires of the cars, but after a while that stopped. We had worn them down. So he was going so fast, I could barely keep up. Sweat poured out of every pore and I coughed stuff out my lungs I didn't even know I had. After about ten revolutions of this, he started to slow down until what seemed an eternity, or did he push me so far until my heart was going to burst, he finally stopped. I unattached the belt from the car and ripped the shorts off. I peed all over myself.

Rufus screamed, "You better have not peed on those shoes. I'll make you lick it off."

Oh, sure, now he wanted to play. I fell to my knees exhausted. He took the shoes and socks off my feet, smelled them to see they were okay and threw all the stuff in the car. He screamed at me to get and after kicking me in the side I did. He handcuffed me to the back of the car and made me walk behind the car back to the farm.

Rufus unattached me from the back bumper and leads me into an outdoor shower house. He shoves into a cement stall with nothing but a series of eyehooks in the wall.

"Shower before bed, slave. We keep clean inside and out," he explains as he grabs a fire hose behind himself and turns the water on. I receive the coldest damn shower of my life. He stops log enough to grab a bottle of sot soap and scrubbing into every pore of me with a horse brush. Then back to the fire hose.

I'm standing there wet and cold when he orders me to push my ass forward. He explains that he is grabbing a bottle of prepared j-like. It's not for me. "It's for the hose that's going up my fat worthless butt."

Somehow he warmed up the water, but I can now say I know what is like for a car getting power washed. The water came out of my ass with the force that it went in and after a couple minutes you could say I was squeaky clean inside and out. Only then did Rufus unattaches the handcuffs and threw me a ruff towel to dry off with. As I bent over he slapped my ass again and spun me around.

"Now listen to me, slave. You will be here 90 days. During that time we will take your soft flabby body and begin to turn it magnificent. You will do as we say. At the end of 90 days, you have a choice – to join our stable of muscleboys and to continue to become a specimen other Masters only dream of and serve two Masters better than all of them put together or to go back to your drunken, smoky, pathetic life."

Rufus pushes me out of the shower room and toward a small cabin on the property. He explains this is the dormitory and the slave I met last night named timothy is waiting for me.

"Timothy has been here the longest. He is your big brother. Do what he says. He knows what must be done. Do you're best slave. If you don't, he gets punished too."

He shoves me in the door and I here the lock click shut.

Instead of sterile white it's shades of hunter green, brown and tan. It looks like a cabin at any cabin summer camp. On either side is a long row of bunks. Must be twelve of them here. Each one is filled except for the last three on the right. Each one has a labeled name burned in wood and a slave in it sound asleep. Two empty bunks and then there is my name on a piece of computer paper taped to the front. None of my stuff can be seen, but sitting smiling on the top bunk is the same muscleboy I saw earlier.

I whisper, "You must be Timothy". Actually I had read his sign.

"Hi little brother." It was at that moment I realized he was the one I slept in his arms the night before.

"Time for bed. We'll talk in the morning. See you at 5 AM."

5 AM? You have go to be kidding I wanted to protest but still I stripped out of the wet jock, hung it over the end of the bed and collapsed into deep sleep.

5 AM comes too quickly. Timothy was shaking me violently telling me to get up, grab my jock and get in line. After making my bed with fastest example of army bunk making with hospital corners I have ever seen he told me to stand next to him.

"Feet together, stomach in, chest out. Don't forget. End every sentence with the word "Sir". Always look them in the eyes. They hate when a slave can't look them in the eye."

I did what I was told just in time, because as Rufus and Gerhard walked in the door, they both stripped to the waist as the tops of their overalls hung behind them. The boots weren't a issue though. They wore thigh high lace-up Wescos.

Gerhard spoke first. "Morning, slaves."

"Morning, Master." They intoned in chorus.

"We have a new one today." I didn't look at him. Didn't even move. "That pig is slave stephen."

134

The whole intones, "Hello, slave stephen."

Timothy kicks me and whispers, "Say 'hello Masters and slave brothers'".

My mind went blanket. He said it again. I took deep breath and said, "Morning Masters and slave brothers."

Gerhard walk over and patted Timothy on the head.

"Keep it up slave. This one is going to be a lot of work."

Timothy kicks me. I remember what he said that light so I answer, "Yes, Sir."

Rufus blares of the hallway. "Morning chores, pigs. To your stations. You have five minutes. Move!"

The slaves scrambled in all different directions. Timothy pushed me in front of him and told me to get going.

When he finally stopped, I asked him what was going on. "Today, I feed the chickens and you're helping. Each slave takes a rotation each day. Today, I have the chickens. There's mucking out the pigs, grooming the horses, milking the cow, cleaning the manure and then all the household duties."

"So what do the Masters do? They pay the bills and help sometimes of it as they feel like it. They're competitive bodybuilders so sometimes they are gone. We make sure that everything runs perfectly in their absence. They pay the bills and play with us when we deserve it."

"What do you mean play with us when we deserve it."

"Don't worry. They are kinky as the day is long." Timothy hands me a shoulder bag full of grain and points me toward the yard. "You'll find out."

He shows me how to scatter the grain.

"What do you mean I'll find out?"

"They only dress that way when new meat arrives and his training begins."

"So how come nothing's happen so far."

"Because they are figuring out the data and sample they took yesterday and devising the fitness plan to get you to the musculature which you will become."

"Really?"

"If you ever wanted to get into shape and be totally owned this is your chance, don't blow it."

"And my stuff?"

"It's in a box with your name on it. They put it in storage and give it back to you dry-cleaned. You will have more cash in your wallet then when you got here. If you decide to stay, one of them goes back with you decides what the house needs and you get to keep and dispose of everything else."

"How do they dispose of it?"

"Ebay and a massive garage sale."

"And they take the money."

"Nope. We open an IRA and there it sits. The Masters put a certain amount into each account based on how hard we work and how much money the farm makes."

Timothy shows me how to refill my bag.

"How long have you been here?"

"Ten. Twelve years."

"And your family and friends. My parents are dead but plenty of the slaves go home for the holidays."

"But my job. My apartment."

The Masters will take care of all of it.

So I did what I was I told. After a few days, I go the hang of life on the farm and even became friends with a few of the other slaves. Timothy turned out to be a good guy even if he was a bit of a mother hen at times. Amazing how you can get used to anything. In bed by 8 and up at 5. Timothy nursed me through some very nasty coughing jags and episodes of nicotine withdrawal but after a couple weeks those subsided and I felt the clean country air fill my body. I started to wonder what I had seen in any of my nasty habits before like drinking, junk food, poppers, and especially smoking. It was at the weekly weigh-in that I got my first show of approval from Master Rufus.

"Slaves, slave stephen, has lost total of 20 pounds. Good, slave."

I glared up at the scale.

"Does slave doubt my word."

I bent down and kissed his boots. He laughed.

"There's plenty of time for that. Back in line."

Later that day, Master Gerhard invited me back into the sterile white room with the gym equipment. He offered me a chair, but I knew better by then and sat on the floor. He came around and sat on the desk.

"All your initial tests came back clean except for high blood pressure and cholesterol. You will be happy to know that the test we did are much better. Your first month here has shown great improvement physically. Your muscle tone has increased and your tests show your cholesterol under control, your blood sugar normal, and normal blood pressure. I think you're hard work deserves something. Clean out the slaves bathroom and meet me in the kitchen at 17:00 Hours."

I smiled and answered, "Yes Sir."

I was there 5 PM on the dot. Master Gerhard grabbed me by the hand and lead me back down the stairs. He wore nothing but his lace-up Wescos and a leather jock. When I go to the bottom, Master Rufus was wearing the same. Master Gerhard ordered me to kneel and walked over to Master Rufus. He drew him close shove his tongue down the black man's throat. Before, I knew it the jocks were off and things were getting hot and heavy. Both of them had huge cocks. It was like looking at models from Tom of Finland picture making it in front of you. They turn and grab me by the arms. I am thrown up against the cross with Master Rufus that they were intending to leave their mark on me. That night Master Rufus whipped me with an inch of my life. It was long, painful, bloody and I loved it. After he cleaned me, I was bent over a spanking bench where Master Gustave spanked me red until my ass blazed heat. They were so impressed with me they said, that I was allowed to touch my cock. I touch it and with one stoke came all over the Masters' boots which I was then required to lick up. The both took turns fucking me.

They were gentle at first and then both ended up riding me mercilessly until they both covered me in cum.

After a shower, which I go to share with the both of them make sure every inch of their bodies was soapy and then clean, Master Gerhard took me to bed and tucked me in kissing me on the forehead before he turned and left. His large cock flopped in the wind of the night and the view of his magnificent ass got me all hard all over again.

They played with me once more before the month was over. I got flogged by Master Gustave this time on both my front and back and then fucked mercilessly again. I was even allowed the honor of sleeping chained to their bed that night. I don't know where they get the energy because they had sex again after "putting me to bed".

Soon the month was over. I had slopped pigs, learned how to groom a horse, and all other the farm tasks as efficiently as the other slaves.

Master Rufus pulled me out of line the next morning and I was ordered back to the white barn room.

Before either of them spoke, I did the only thing I could think of doing. It was 90 days. Timothy had reminded me enough it was coming up.

I got on my knees and with tears welling in my eyes, I begged to stay.

My mother enjoyed meeting Master Gustav and she was shocked with the difference in me. The workouts, the farm living, and the clean living had changed me. My mother was shocked when I held her chair out for her. She kept asking if I had joined the military. This pleased Master very much. We took care of all my affairs. But I wanted one last thing and he agreed.

Mark didn't even recognize me. A bottle of water at my favorite leather bar. I got us both bottles of water. I didn't have to look for Master. The pinball machine rang out from behind me.

THE PURIFICATION

Emerging from separate doors in the corners of room, two priests, dressed in long black robes that gently float behind them as they glide down the church aisles, shake the shining thirofurs from their long silver chains with long fluid strokes leaving trails of long white smoke behind themselves. The smoke sweeps its way circling through the air and on to the fog-laden floor.

No outsider had been allowed into their rituals, but I with my hidden camera, decided to try. The last reporter sent, Henry Stuckman, had told me about rituals of sacrifice and other strange practices, but as soon as he was ready to submit the first of his articles, he vanished. His blonde bimbo roommate said that he had not come home for several days. She said this as a very sad little girl. The look on her face complete with a pout as she dragged her pinky in between her large, silicon breasts. A waste of effort probably meant purely for my enticement and entertainment.

As the priest reached the altar, they turned off, each standing in a far corner in the front of the church. In its glory days, the place had been know as St. Aloysius, but declining congregations and all too many lawsuits for inappropriate priests behavior later. The Archdiocese declared in too much disrepair, which it was not, and declared it closed. They probably thought they had sold it off to another Christian sect. Once this story hit the paper, they would have the Cardinal make some lame excuse about being lied to. No one including religious and political leaders in this day and age take responsibilities for their screw-ups except newspapermen and we get ours crammed down our throats by our colleagues, editors, and publishers.

I crept slowly behind the very neatly dressed crowd. If seen going in it look like any WASPish congregation in suits and ties. The ladies were dressed in very old-fashioned Sunday best. No dress was above the knee and all were brightly colored. Each lady clasped a large floppy hat with a colored ribbon hanging from. One row had hats with red ribbons and the on behind had ribbons of blue. The other thing I noticed upon entering is that all the women were seated together in the back pews while the men were together in the front. The men spoke from time to time but against what I would have thought was their nature the ladies sat in wrapped attention with their hands and hats neatly on their laps and without a word passing their lips even while the men prayed out loud.

I crept behind a group of other men in the back of the room until I could see the altar. These men were all dressed differently and many didn't seem to know the prayers yet.

The heavy oak doors to the church flew open with a bang. In the doorway stood two muscular body builders. Every sinew of their muscles could be seen traced in the hairless of their bodies. No robes for these men. They were dressed in leather gladiator uniforms complete with roman lace-up sandals laced up to their huge thighs. Their great arms were crossed as if daring anyone to approach the individual between them. He I draped in white linen from head to town. The enveloping garment covered his head in a hood and hid where extremities stopped. His head was bowed and his arms neatly at his side.

From behind me, there was a great explosion. I jerked my head to see a large bull of a man rising from a hole on to the altar. He is dressed in a black leather vest, harness, chaps and Wescos. He emerges from a great cloud of smoke. The smoke slowly disappears. His muscles and shoulder width was greater than the gladiators were and his chest was a matte of fur. His blue eyes pierced right through you. He commanded absolute submission before he uttered a single word.

He reached out with his mighty arm and motions the three forward. The white clad figure pulls back his hood. He was a boy maybe 24 or 25. From his shoulders, he allows the white robe to slip and hit the floor. He has already worked out for many years because with the firmness of youth comes with great musculature. He wears only a black leather thong that bulges to barely contain what is within. With smallest movement of his index figure, the great figure motions the boy forward. The boy steps out the robe and walks slowly down the aisle. The musclemen following like two large lumbering apes.

The boy's blonde curls bounce as he slowly makes his way down to the foot of the altar. A few feet short he stops. The bass voice of the great man speaks, "Are you ready to except which in your word of honor you said was your destiny?"

The boy bows his head and murmurs.

"Louder so all can here!"

The boy looks up and with no emotion in his eyes says, "I am".

"Then, kneel!"

The boy slowly sinks down on his knees as the great man approaches the end of the altar. He needs no microphone to be heard.

"Patrick, for someone so young you have shown great strength and intelligence. My first impulses are look at someone like you and instantly enslave them because usually they do not have the strength of character and technique to be worth to be one of us. Patrick, are you ready to be one of the rulers instead of one of the ruled?"

Patrick arises back to his feet. And returns the great one's stony stare.

His hands at his side with his fists clenched.

"Yes Sir. I am Sir!"

"Then Patrick turn to what was your betters and receive your leathers."

The priests who had earlier stunk the place up with their incense return each with a few articles of leather. To this boy's body, they add a harness, chaps, vest, Wescos to the knee and finally a Master's cap. The leathers clung to the features of his young, smooth, masculine body.

"Let is all be known that from now this is Master Patrick and he has earned his right to be one of us with all respect and privileges that go with the title."

The men around me cheer. The suited men stand up and cheer, whoop, and hollered as well. The ladies did not move.

"Silence!"

The great man's arm swept the room and all reverie suddenly stopped. The suited men straighten their suits and returned to their seats. The ladies still did not move.

The great man walk to the stairs of the altar.

"Come Master Patrick and be seated while we enslave some of the other members of your class."

Master Patrick comes up to the altar sits in a large black leather chair in the back of the altar.

"Guards! Bring them forward!"

The two big apes disappear only to reappear in a couple moments equipped with long black single tails in their hands beating forward a shivering hairless mass of maybe twenty men who are chained together neck, wrist and foot in heavy black shackles. Their hairlessness is almost complete. I think they only hair they had is their eyebrows.

"Bring the slaves down and turn them to face the pews."

This the two big apes did whipping the random hapless slave who wasn't moving fast enough.

The slaves were lined up and instead of being ordered to bow, the ape kick each slave behind the knees forcing them painfully down to the floor.

"No complaints? Excellent slaves. Men look. These are new playthings. Do them what you please. But remember, what you play with today will be played with by someone else tomorrow. Do not break the toys!"

I whispered to the guy next to me, "What happens when break the toys?"

The man turned to me. His eyes opened wide and he held his breath and he looked back at the stage.

I must have heard because we got the full attention of the great man on stage.

"Gentlemen, what you have seen is the end of a great journey that all these men of honor agreed to take. Think very hard about your next move."

And with that last statement, the great man turns his well-muscled furry ass and vanishes back down in the altar in another cloud of smoke.

No one moves. Master Patrick walks off the altar and up to the slaves. He points at a slight older but totally tan, slim and tightly muscular one. The apes unhook him from the rest and give Master Patrick the end of his neck chain. Patrick pulls him forward and spits full on in his face.

"Don't make me tell you to move again. When in my presence you better be on your feet and ready for anything, slave." He yanks on the slave's chain a couple of times and then drags him to the front of the church. I turn to look but they seem to disappear before they even reach the front door.

Each row of the pews gets out orderly taking turns as they leave. Some stop to take a slave, while others exit the church. Finally it is the ladies turn to leave. The last suited man motions and they rise filling out of the church in single file. Then it was our turn to leave. As we reached the church doors, they close with a clang. The great one in his furry muscular glory stands between freedom and us.

"Who spoke?"

We all stand looking at each other dumbfounded.

"You wanted to know what happened to one who failed."

As if we were on an elementary school playground, the guy who smirked back at me points with his arm straight at me.

"Walk forward, neophyte."

My first thought was "Oh, shit". Here I had been doing my best to be inconspicuous and my big mouth had got me in trouble again.

"Are you serious about the journey?"

If I was going to get this story, I better play along.

"I...I don't know, your Excellency."

"You must wish to explore. You must have a thirst to know more."

The more a new a better news story it would be. I bowed my head. "Yes, Sir, I wish to know more."

"A slave?"

I took as a step back and panicked. I had seen those poor naked souls. I sure as hell didn't want to be one of them. "Um, No Sir. I mean 'no'."

He walked closer to me. "So think you have what it takes to be one of us?"

I looked him straight in the eye. "Yes, Sir."

"That's better." He smiles. "But we'll find out. Until you finish our training you don't really know. You may have a power that goes beyond what you could have ever dreamed. Or you may be one of many want to be in our gay world."

"You are all gay."

"Aren't you?"

"Hell yeah."

"What's the problem?"

"Then what are the broads for?"

"They're not women. They weren't born that way. The red ribbons were top applicants and the blue ribbons were slave applicants. In this place, failure comes with consequences."

He glances around to the group. "So does noisiness." The newest blue ribbon is a reporter who thought he could tell all about something which is only our business."

The apes reappeared. "Think carefully. You have a day. We know where you are every minute of every day. Make your decision. If you are not here tomorrow at 6 p.m. sharp. We will come for you."

The apes push open the door. My fellow men walk slowly out to the door. He caught me by the arm. "Think carefully."

I walked out of the church with my mind whirling. I walked down a couple blocks and shut my hat camera off and the tape recorder in my suit pocket. I could blow the doors off this so-called church now but for completeness and perhaps my own safety, I wouldn't want to piss someone the size of the great ones and the apes off, I'd return tomorrow at 6. I couldn't wait to return the next day.

By 5:58, the same group of men I stood with the day before were assembled on the foot of the church. My hat camera was loaded with a new load of film. The apes open the doors with a slam and drag the first of us into the doors. The rest follow.

We don't turn into the sanctuary, but into a hallway behind a hard walnut door next to the entrance. The apes lead us forth and down into the bowels of the church. The stairway down is made of short stairs and we are constantly bumping against each other as we descend down. The room is dark except for spotty wall lamps and dark except for the movement of us down the stairs.

At the bottom, the apes drag us forward and shut out the last of the light to leave us in total darkness. The men behind me begin to shuffle. The apes are pushing us forward. I begin to move forward in baby steps. My eyes try to adjust to the light, but all I can see is shadows of primarily shaped objects with no features other than shape to differentiate them. I feel along the wall and feel a sconce saying that we are moving into another room. The smell of moisture hits my nostrils. A little appears below another door in front of us. One of the apes lumbers forward and opens the door. Light fills the room we are in and I can see that we are walking through a small storage room. To my right is a small contraption, a hydraulic lift. Underneath is a small refrigerator with the warning sticker, "Beware-dry ice". Guess that's showbiz, folks. The apes top us at the entrance and order us to disrobe. On the wall are several hooks. We'll there goes my camera. The men around me undressed so quickly, I had a hard time keeping up. When we were all naked, the apes pushed us in one by one. I didn't even have time to check out the other men.

The light blinds me as I enter the room. When I say this room was white it was almost sterilely so. The room was absolutely white from the light to the walls to every corner and crevice. The room was far from a blank. It was filled with rows of ancient Greek columns mixed with white flowers and sculptures of ancient pyramids. The only color in the room were the inhabitants in it and the blue of a pool of water off to my right. The pool itself was stark white, which further emphasized the blue of the clear water within it.

We were far from alone in the room. The apes had disappeared closing the doors behind him. The open we had come into was now just part of the walls. A neat row of five naked shaved slaves kneeled at the head of the pool wearing only white colors that shined in the light. I look around to my fellow men. Most weren't in bad shape. Some were bearish and a couple were honestly gym bunnies.

I looked back at the pool and the slaves had been joined by a man all in white latex wearing a long white latex cloak. My cock began to rise. Though I could not see his face for his head was covered in a white latex mask, the rubber highlight a massive muscular frame every inch solid muscle and a large cock hung down his rubber clad leg. It was obviously uncut. Okay. I was forgetting I was on assignment, but he was beautiful covered in a complete white latex loveliness. He held his hands out to us.

"Do not fear neophytes for you have made it this far."

He spoke in whisper but in the room it was more than loud enough. It was obvious he wanted to assure us, and his manner did that all too well for him.

"If you are ready, tonight you will begin your journey to the brotherhood and be purified. This is the water that binds us all. It is our first step, before we lose our body hair but with it our trepidation, fear, loneliness, and embrace a road to make us as men more complete."

As I stand here, I watch my brethren. A slave comes down and while the man in white latex watches they lead him to the pool. The man beckons them to enter and immerse themselves in the water. He blesses them which what I recognize is the Hebrew prayer of thanks. The man arises and the slave leads him into a room beyond the white room opposite from where we came in. The slave returns alone.

Now it is my turn. My cock by this time is rock hard and I try to cover it up. The man in the white lets out a little chuckle at my sheepishness. The cock down his leg has hardened as well. It is maybe 10-12 inches and almost down to his knee.

"Are you prepared my brother to be?"

My mind is exploding. Run. You've got more than enough for this story. You are screwing with these people's spirituality. Run. Something stops me. My brain says run but my soul tells me to open up and accept what I am being given. My soul wins and I slowly go down the stairs into the water.

The prayer begins. I walk don the stairs into a pool much deeper than expected. I close my eyes and hold my breath. From above, a light touch taps my head to keep me down. Several seconds later, the hand moves to my chin to pull me back up. I open my eyes underwater. My eyes didn't burn. The water is clean and clear. The slaves and the man in white look down upon me like Gods from Olympus. One of the slave's hands breaks through the surface of the water and guides to me to the top of the stairs.

As I emerge all thoughts are gone. I feel a purity of spirit and cleanliness of mind and boy and for the first time in a long time, peace.

The slave does not let me go but leads me dripping across the room and beyond the door. Another pair of slaves with white collars rough dry me off and I am lead to a large slave. He is the size of a football linebacker. In his hands a gleaning silver shaver. Is this where Henry freaked? Is this when they found out? I didn't care. I was laid back on a stark white table with a hole on the top of it. Underneath the whole was a bucket. One slave on the side was sweeping up a pile of multi colored hairs. The razor went through what hair I did have on top of my head which to be honest wasn't much. I always wanted to see what I would be like bald and now I was going to find out first hand.

ABOUT THE AUTHOR

Markus Larsen, the kinky cub has been in the
leather community close to three decades. He is a
co-founder of the nation's premiere Leather Boys
Clubs and is a member of organizations as diverse
as Mystery Writers of America and the Chicago
Hellfire Club. The cub hopes to not only excite
but hopes you will have a great time reading this
collection – his first.

www.ingramcontent.com/pod-product-compliance
Lightning Source LLC
Chambersburg PA
CBHW071228260626
47162CB00004B/1459